力得文化
Leader Culture

開啟職場
字彙
聯想力

力得編輯群 ◎著

別再糾結背單字這件小事啦！
不是背不住單字，是不曉得該怎麼背！

特別企劃 **4** 大主題，分 **48** 個單元，教你
這樣看：單字**主題分類**，查找不麻煩！
這樣唸：專業美籍外師**親自錄製MP3**！
這樣用：隨字搭配例句，字彙應用好輕鬆！

一次就搞定
【職業與公司】、【國家與新聞】】、【交通與房地產】、【科技與科學】
英文字彙！

MP3

編者序

　　一般大家比較熟悉的英文單字背法即是：買一本單字書，由Ａ到Ｚ依序往下背的填鴨式記憶法。往往很多讀者會遇到的情況是，單字記住了，卻不曉得該如何用、在哪裡用。更有人是，看到一半，覺得單字太多、時間不夠，索性放棄。

　　本書整理了４大方向的與職場相關的常用單字，依主題分類，讓讀者輕鬆吸收英文字彙，另附美籍老師錄製的MP3，方便讀者邊聽、邊看、邊學、邊記憶。期許讀者學英文之路順遂。

編輯部

Contents
目次

主題 **2** 國家與新聞

主題 3　交通與房地產

主題 4　科技與科學

主題 1

Occupation & Company

職業與公司

School 學校

Track 01

1 **education** [ˌɛdʒʊˋkeʃən] *n.* 教育；訓導；教育學

Education should be geared to children's needs and abilities.
教育應適應兒童的需要和能力。
compulsory education 義務教育
higher education 高等教育

2 **staff** [stæf] *n.* 工作人員；參謀

It was arranged that my staff would meet you at the station.
已經安排好我的員工在車站等你。

3 **director** [dəˋrɛktɚ] *n.* 指導者；理事；導演

Do not go against the director.
不要和導演作對。
a film director 電影導演

4 **headmaster** [ˋhɛdˋmæstɚ] *n.* 校長

The headmaster made a speech at graduation.
校長在畢業典禮上發表演說。

5 **dean** [din] *n.* （大學）院長，系主任

Ms. Cook will be the dean of our department next

semester.

庫克女士下學期將會擔任我們的系主任。

6　teacher　[ˋtitʃɚ]　*n.*　教師

I asked the teacher for her advice.

我徵求這位老師的意見。

a qualified teacher 合格教師

high school teacher 中學老師

a history/geography teacher 歷史／地理老師

7　schoolmaster　[ˋskul͵mæstɚ]　*n.*　（男）教師；校長

She was village schoolmaster for several years.

她當了好幾年的鄉村小學的校長。

8　assistant　[əˋsɪstənt]　*n.*　助手，助理；助教

He worked as an assistant to the President.

他當過總統助理。

【同】affiliate, confederate

9　tutor　[ˋtjutɚ]　*n.*　家庭教師；導師　*vi.*　當家庭教師

Many college students tutor after class.

很多大學生課後接家教。

【同】teacher, instructor, coach

10　enroll　[ɪnˋrol]　*vt.*　登記，招收　*vi.*　參軍

All contestants must enroll by Saturday.

所有參賽者必須在星期六前登記。

【同】enlist, register, recruit

11 **pupil**　　[ˋpjup!]　　*n.*　　小學生；學生

The school has 600 pupils.

這所學校有六百名小學生。

pupil 還有另外一個解釋，就是「瞳孔」，要記起來哦！

12 **student**　　[ˋstjudnt]　　*n.*　　學生

It is student's duty to study hard.

學生的本分是用功念書。

a student loan 學生貸款

high school student 中學生

13 **scholar**　　[ˋskɑlɚ]　　*n.*　　學者；獎學金獲得者

My professor is an outstanding scholar.

我的教授是一名傑出的學者。

scholarship　*n.*　獎學金

14 **playground**　　[ˋpleˏɡraʊnd]　　*n.*　　操場，運動場

You can find him on the playground, I think.

我想你去操場能找到他。

15 **gymnasium**　　[dʒɪmˋnezɪəm]　　*n.*　　體育館，健身房

My friends and I often go to the gymnasium after school.

我和我朋友常常放學後去體育館。

16 **learning**　　[ˋlɝnɪŋ]　　*n.*　　學習；學問，知識

A little learning is a dangerous thing.

【諺】一知半解，危害不淺。

language learning 語言學習

17 **extraordinary**　[ɪk`strɔrdn͵ɛrɪ]　*adj.*　非同尋常的，特別

This novel shares the author's extraordinary experience.

這本小說分享了作者特別的經驗。

18 **diligent**　[`dɪlədʒənt]　*adj.*　勤勉的，勤奮的

Miranda is a diligent student.

米蘭達是勤勉的學生。

19 **progress**　[prə`grɛs]　*n.*　前進，進展；進步

She keeps making progress in learning.

她在學習上持續進步。

make better progress 取得了較好的進步

make great progress 取得非常大的進步

20 **exceptional**　[ɪk`sɛpʃən!]　*adj.*　例外的；優越的

They are exceptional students.

他們是優秀的學生。

21 **university**　[͵junə`vɝsətɪ]　*n.*　綜合性大學

My uncle is a professor at this university.

我的伯父是這所大學的一名教授。

Beijing has hundreds of universities.

北京有幾百所大學。

He is a university teacher.

他是一個大學教師。

22 **enlighten** [ɪnˋlaɪtn] *vt.* 啟發，開導；啟蒙

The teacher enlightened her students on developing their potential.

這個老師啟蒙她的學生開發他們的潛力。

【同】instruct, illuminate

【反】confuse, bewilder

23 **impart** [ɪmˋpɑrt] *vt.* 給予，傳遞；告訴

The aim of the course is to impart the importance of critical thinking.

這門課的目標旨在傳授批判性思考的重要。

【同】inform, reveal

【反】conceal

24 **lecture** [ˋlɛktʃɚ] *n.* *vi.* 演講，講課

The students preview the paper before having the lecture.

學生在上課前預習論文。

【同】speech, lesson

25 **instruct** [ɪnˋstrʌkt] *vt.* 教；指示；通知

My job is to instruct her in English.

我的工作是教她英語。

26 **method** [ˋmɛθəd] *n.* 方法，辦法；教學法

I have a simple and easy method.
我有個簡易的方法。
a new method of teaching English
一個教英語的新方法
a man of method
有條理的人

27 subject　　[`sʌbdʒɪkt]　*n.*　題目；學科；主語

How many subjects are you studying this semester?
這學期你選了幾門課程？
the subject of this sentence
這個句子的主語

28 profound　　[prə`faʊnd]　*adj.*　深刻的；淵博的

My father has a profound influence on my creation.
我爸爸對我的創作有很大的影響。

29 experience　　[ɪk`spɪrɪəns]　*n.*　經驗，感受；經歷

I had no work experience when I just graduated from college.
我大學剛畢業時，完全沒有工作經驗。
Experience is the best teacher.
【諺】經驗是最好的老師。

30 preside　　[prɪ`zaɪd]　*vi.*　主持；主奏

The manager presided at the meeting.
經理主持會議。

Medical 醫療

 Track 02

1　nurse　[nɝs]　*n.*　護士

My classmate dreams of becoming a nurse.

我的同學夢想成為一名護士。

a licensed nurse 有執照的護士

2　needle　[ˋnidl̩]　*n.*　針，縫補，編織針

His right foot was pierced by a needle.

他的右腳被針刺到。

a needle and thread 針線

3　prick　[prɪk]　*vt.*　刺（穿）　*n.*　刺孔

She got her finger pricked by a thorn.

她的手指被刺紮了一下。

4　stick　[stɪk]　*vt.*　*vi.*　伸，伸出

Don't stick your head out of the train window.

不要把頭伸出火車窗外面。

relay stick 接力棒

stick to 堅持，固守

5　blood　[blʌd]　*n.*　血

Lots of people donated blood.

許多人捐血。

high/low blood pressure 高／低血壓

6　**patient**　[ˋpeʃənt]　*adj.*　忍耐的　*n.*　病人

The patient has no appetite for food.

這個病人對食物沒胃口。

He is patient of noises.

他一直忍耐著噪音。

The patient is getting better.

那位患者漸漸好轉。

7　**disease**　[dɪˋziz]　*n.*　疾病

He is diagnosed as having an unknown disease.

他被診斷出罹患不知名的疾病。

a heart disease 心臟病

8　**illness**　[ˋɪlnɪs]　*n.*　病，疾病

She went to work despite her illness.

儘管生病，她還是去上班。

【同】sickness, disease

【反】health

9　**room**　[rum]　*n.*　房間

The parents decorate the room with dolls.

這對父母用布偶佈置房間。

reading room 閱覽室

waiting room 候車（診）室

10 **bed** [bɛd] *n.* 床

Life isn't a bed of roses.

【諺】人生並非事事稱心如意。

go to bed 睡覺；就寢

make the bed 整理床鋪

11 **asleep** [ə`slip] *adj.* 睡著的，睡熟的

The little boy soon fell asleep after having dinner.

小男孩吃過晚餐後，很快就睡著了。

fall asleep 入睡、睡著

sound asleep 睡得很熟

12 **visitor** [`vɪzɪtɚ] *n.* 訪問者；參觀者

There are many visitors to the White House every year.

每年參觀白宮的遊客很多。

visitor's book 來客留言簿

13 **recover** [rɪ`kʌvɚ] *vt.* 重新獲得；挽回

The patient made a great effort to recover from her illness.

那位病患努力讓她自己恢復健康。

be recovered 恢復健康

14 **doctor** [`dɑktɚ] *n.* 醫生，醫師；博士

The doctor examined the child's throat.

醫生檢查這個小孩的喉嚨。

see a doctor 看醫生

15 **treat**   [trit]   *vt.*   治療

The doctor cannot refuse to treat any patient.

醫生不能拒絕醫治任何病人。

be treated as 作為……對待

treat...as... 對待……作為……

16 **operation**   [ˌɑpəˋreʃən]   *n.*   運算

The surgeon has performed the operation.

外科醫生做了手術。

have an operation for 對……做手術

17 **anatomy**   [əˋnætəmɪ]   *n.*   解剖

He is a professor of anatomy in college.

他是大學的解剖學教授。

18 **medicine**   [ˋmɛdəsn]   *n.*   醫學；內科學

There have been great advances in medicine in the last ten years.

在過去十年裡，醫學有了極大的進步。

give sb. some medicine 給某人一些藥

have (take) this medicine 吃這種藥

19 **drug**   [drʌg]   *n.*   藥，藥物，藥材

Please take the drug on prescription.

請憑處方服藥。

take the drug 服藥

20 **care** [kɛr] *n.* 照料；保護；小心

The baby needs a lot of care.
這嬰孩需要很多照料。
Take care! 小心！
take care of 照顧、照料

21 **stricken** [`strɪkən] *adj.* 受傷的；受挫的

The stricken were sent to the hospital.
受傷的人被送去醫院。

22 **hospital** [`hɑspɪt!] *n.* 醫院

She works at the hospital.
她在醫院工作。

23 **large** [lɑrdʒ] *adj.* 大的；巨大的

Shanghai is a large city.
上海是一個大城市。
a large family 大家庭

24 **busy** [`bɪzɪ] *adj.* 忙的；繁忙的

He is busy chatting with his girlfriend.
他正忙著和女朋友聊天。
be busy doing sth. 忙於做某事
be busy with sth. 忙於做某事

25 ward   [wɔrd]   *n.*   病房，病室；監房

This pregnant woman was put in a maternity ward.

這名孕婦住進了產科病房。

26 mental   [`mɛnt!]   *adj.*   精神的；腦力的

Her problem is mental, not physical.

她的毛病是精神方面的，而不是身體方面的。

27 voluntary   [`vɑlən,tɛrɪ]   *adj.*   自願的，志願的

She used to do voluntary work every day.

她過去天天做志願服務。

28 insurance   [ɪn`ʃʊrəns]   *n.*   保險；保險費

I am an insurance broker.

我是一名保險經紀人。

29 bill   [bɪl]   *n.*   帳單；招貼；票據

I can't pay now; please bill me later.

我現在不能付款，請以後開帳單給我。

30 pay   [pe]   *vt.*   給……報酬   *n.*   工資

He gets his pay each Friday.

他每星期五領工資。

pay for sth. 付錢，支付，付出代價

pay sb. 付某人錢

Sports 運動

 Track 03

1 coach   [kotʃ]   *vt.*   輔導，指導，訓練   *n.*   教練

He is not so much a player as a coach.

與其說他是個隊員，不如說他是個教練。

career coach 就業顧問師

coach party 巴士旅行團

2 whistle   [`hwɪs!]   *n.*   口哨聲   *vi.*   吹口哨

The kid was forbidden to whistle at night.

這小孩被禁止在夜裡吹口哨。

3 clock   [klɑk]   *n.*   鐘，儀錶

The clock shows half past two.

時鐘的針指著兩點半。

the alarm clock 鬧鐘

body clock 生理時鐘

4 time   [taɪm]   *n.*   時間

Time is money.

【諺】時間就是金錢。

all the time 一直；始終

on time 準時；不早不晚

5 **quarter** [ˋkwɔrtɚ] *n.* 四分之一；一刻鐘

It's a quarter past ten.

現在是十點一刻。

a quarter to six 差一刻六點

a quarter past six 六點一刻

6 **player** [ˋpleɚ] *n.* 比賽者，選手

He is a skillful football player.

他足球踢得很好。

player piano 自動演奏的鋼琴

7 **basketball** [ˋbæskɪt͵bɔl] *n.* 籃球；籃球運動

My brother likes to play basketball after school.

我弟弟放學後喜歡打籃球。

8 **sweat** [swɛt] n. 汗

He is covered with sweat.

他渾身是汗。

a cold sweat 冷汗

break (out) into a sweat 變得很緊張

9 **shoot** [ʃut] *vt.* 發射；射中 *n.* 發芽

He shot a wild duck.

他射中一隻野鴨。

shot down 擊落

shoot-off 延長比賽

10 ball [bɔl] *n.* 球

He hit the tennis ball over the net.
他把網球打過了網。

11 baseball [`bes,bɔl] *n.* 棒球；棒球運動

I enjoy watching baseball games with my dad.
我喜歡和爸爸看棒球賽轉播。

baseball cap 棒球帽

12 throw [θro] *vt.* *vi.* 投擲；摔倒

He threw the stone in the air.
他把石頭拋向空中。

throw off 扔下
throw up 吐出（食物）、嘔吐

13 hit [hɪt] *vt.* 打；擊中；撞

The dog was hit by a car accidentally.
這隻狗意外被車撞。

hit on the head with sth. 用某東西打在頭上
be hit in the face 被打在臉上

14 double [`dʌb!] *adj.* 兩倍的；雙的

The egg has a double yolk.
這蛋有雙蛋黃。

a double bed 雙人床

15 catch [kætʃ] *vi.* 鈎住；掛住；絆住

The policeman caught the thief.

員警逮住了小偷。

catch a cold 著涼；傷風；感冒

catch up with 趕上（或超過）

16 agent [ˋedʒənt] *n.* 代理人，代理商

I booked my holiday through my local travel agent.

我是由本地的旅遊代理人預先安排的度假事宜。

17 salary [ˋsælərɪ] *n.* 薪金，薪水

I want to speak to her concerning my salary.

我想跟她談談我的薪水問題。

monthly salary 月薪

basic salary 基本薪資

18 commission [kəˋmɪʃən] *n.* 委託，委任；委託狀

Does he take our commission?

他接受我們的委託嗎？

19 team [tim] *n.* 隊 *vi.* 協作，合作

I am on the school football team.

我是學校足球隊的隊員。

be on one's city team 是在城市代表隊

20 goal [gol] *n.* 球門；得分；目的

It's in. We score a goal!

球進了。我們射門得分。

【同】destination, intent, target

21 **soccer** [ˋsɑkɚ] *n.* 英式足球

She has a crush on that boy who is playing soccer.

她暗戀那個現在正在踢足球的男孩。

22 **football** [ˋfʊt͵bɔl] *n.* 足球比賽;足球

Our team has won the football match.

我們隊贏得了足球賽。

23 **everywhere** [ˋɛvrɪ͵hwɛr] *adv.* 到處,無論哪裡

My younger sister used to follow me everywhere I go.

我妹妹過去總跟著我,無論我到哪裡。

look everywhere for you 到處找你

24 **uniform** [ˋjunə͵fɔrm] *adj.* 一樣的 *n.* 制服

Soldiers wear a distinctive uniform.

士兵們穿著特製的制服。

The desks in the office are uniform.

辦公室裡的桌子都一樣。

25 **schedule** [ˋskɛdʒʊl] *n.* 時間表;計畫表

The teacher posted the schedule of classes.

教師將課程表公佈出來了。

【同】timetable, program

26 result　　[rɪˋzʌlt]　*n.*　結果；效果

The result of the match was 2-1 to Chicago.

比賽結果芝加哥隊以二比一獲勝。

as a result of …的結果

result in 導致，結果

27 badminton　　[ˋbædmɪntən]　*n.*　羽毛球

She is good at playing badminton.

她擅長打羽球。

28 net　　[nɛt]　*vt.*　用網捕；用網覆蓋

This area has not been covered by the communication net.

這個地區還不在通訊網的覆蓋之內。

She put a net on her hair.

她在頭髮上放一個網。

fishing nets 漁網

29 athletic　　[æθˋlɛtɪk]　*adj.*　運動的

Athletic sports are good for your health.

體育運動有益健康。

30 sinew　　[ˋsɪnju]　*n.*　腱，力量，精力

The interviewees are all with their sinews tensed.

面試者們全都精神緊繃。

Business 商業

 Track 04

1 **firm** 　[fɝm]　*n.*　商行，商號，公司；嚴格

Parents must be firm with their children.

父母對孩子一定要嚴格。

ring the building firm 給建築公司打電話

2 **enterprise** 　[ˋɛntɚˌpraɪz]　*n.*　艱巨的事業；事業心

The scandal about the enterprise was spread.

關於那家企業的醜聞被散播出來。

【同】company, firm

3 **owner** 　[ˋonɚ]　*n.*　物主，所有人

I am the rightful owner of this car.

我是這輛新車的合法主人。

4 **successor** 　[səkˋsɛsɚ]　*n.*　繼承人，繼任者

The vice president was the president's successor.

副總統是總統的繼任人。

5 **management** 　[ˋmænɪdʒmənt]　*n.*　管理；經營，處理

The manager considers a better way of management in his section.

這位經理思考管理他部門更好的方法。

【同】administration, direction

6 **manager** [`mænɪdʒɚ] *n.* 經理；管理人

Our manager is responsible and invincible.

我們經理既有責任感，又堅強。

bank manager 銀行分行經理

stage manager 舞台監督

7 **manage** [`mænɪdʒ] *vt.* 設法；對付

His wife knows how to manage him when he is angry.

他的妻子知道在他生氣時怎麼對付他。

manage to do sth. 設法做某事

manage it myself 我自己做（處理）它，我自己來

8 **decide** [dɪ`saɪd] *vi. vt.* 下決心；決定

It's difficult to decide between the two.

對這兩者，不易做出抉擇。

decide to do sth. 決定做某事

decide on doing sth. 決心做某事

9 **choose** [tʃuz] *vt. vi.* 選擇

I chose my boyfriend a coat.

我替我男朋友挑了一件外套。

choose sb. (sth.) for... 因……選擇某人（某東西）

choose to do sth. 決定做某事

10 **customer** [ˈkʌstəmə] *n.* 顧客，主顧

She is one of our regular customers.
她是我們的一個好顧客。

11 **client** [ˈklaɪənt] *n.* 顧客；訴訟委託人

The client asks the lawyer to help him.
委託人要求律師幫他。

【同】customer, consumer

12 **assist** [əˈsɪst] *vt.* 援助，幫助；攙扶

I assist her in finishing her homework.
我協助她完成功課。

13 **telephone** [ˈtɛlə,fon] *n.* 電話 *vi.* 打電話

I telephoned to thank my professor.
我打電話向我的教授道謝。

make a telephone (phone) call 打電話

talk with sb. on (over) the telephone 用電話和某人談話

14 **appointment** [əˈpɔɪntmənt] *n.* 任命；約定，約會

I have an appointment with them this weekend.
我這週末與他們有個約會。

15 **clerk** [klɝk] *n.* 辦事員；秘書

My cousin got a job as a bank clerk.
我表哥得到一份銀行職員的工作。

a bank clerk 一個銀行的職員

a city clerk 政府官員

16 program [`progræm] *vi.* 編制程式

What functions can this program perform?

這一程式有哪些功能？

17 stock [stɑk] *n.* 原料；庫存品；股本

The store took stock on Monday.

那家商店每逢星期一進行盤點。

stock control 庫存核算

stock certificate 股票

18 benefit [`bɛnəfɪt] *n.* 利益；恩惠；津貼

This project is of great benefit to everyone.

這項工程對每個人都大有好處。

19 employ [ɪm`plɔɪ] *vi.* 雇用；用；使忙於

He has fifteen workers in his employ.

他雇用的工人有十五名。

20 quit [kwɪt] *vt.* 離開，退出；停止

He quit Paris after a week.

他一週後離開了巴黎。

動詞三態：quit, quit, quit。

21 **retire**   [rɪ`taɪr]   *vi.*   退下;引退;就寢

He retired to bed, but he did not sleep.

他就寢了,但睡不著。

22 **seek**   [sik]   *vt.*   尋找,探索;試圖

They were seeking employment.

他們在找工作。

hide and seek 捉迷藏

23 **find**   [faɪnd]   *v.*   找到;發現

Look what I've found.

瞧我找到什麼了。

find it impossible to do sth. 發現做某事是不可能的

find one's way 努力前進,尋路前進

24 **hurry**   [`hɝɪ]   *vi.*   趕緊   *vt.*   催促

He was in a hurry to leave.

他急切地要離開。

hurry off 匆匆離去;趕快去

hurry up 趕快

25 **friend**   [frɛnd]   *n.*   朋友

A friend in need is a friend indeed.

【諺】患難之交才是真朋友。

be friends with 與⋯⋯要好

make lots of new friends 交許多新朋友

26 associate   [əˋsoʃɪɪt]   *vi.*   交往   *n.*   夥伴，同事

I got a new job and a new set of work associates.

我有了新工作和一班新同事。

27 employee   [ˌɛmplɔɪˋi]   *n.*   受雇者，雇員，雇工

Every employer hopes to find responsible employees.

每個雇主都希望找到負責任的雇員。

28 shrewd   [ʃrud]   *adj.*   判斷敏捷的，精明的

She is a shrewd leader in the party.

她是政黨裡精明的領袖。

【同】astute, judicious

【反】dull, obtuse

29 treaty   [ˋtritɪ]   *n.*   條約；協定，協定

The government plans to sign a peace treaty with its neighbor.

這個政府計畫與鄰國簽署和平協議。

【同】pact, convention, agreement

30 adversary   [ˋædvɚˌsɛrɪ]   *n.*   對手，敵手

He is a respectable adversary.

他是一個值得尊敬的對手。

【同】antagonist, competitor

【反】ally, friend

Blue Collar 藍領

Track 05

1 **build** [bɪld] *vt.* 建築；建立；創立

The house is built of wood.

這房子是用木頭建造的。

Rome was not built in a day.

【諺】羅馬不是一天建成的。

be built of 用……製造

2 **pipe** [paɪp] *n.* 管子，導管，輸送管

Get the plumber to fix the leaky pipe.

找水電工來修漏水的管子。

The main gas pipe burst.

瓦斯的主要管道破了。

a collection of rare pipes 珍奇煙斗的收集品

3 **connect** [kə`nɛkt] *vt.* 連接，聯結；聯繫

The plumber connected up all the pipes and turned on the tap.

管子工連接上所有管子，然後打開了水龍頭。

4 **leak** [lik] *n.* 漏洞，漏隙

There is a leak in the roof.

屋頂上有個漏洞。

【同】crack, hole

5 **electricity**   [ˌɪlɛk`trɪsətɪ]   *n.*   電，電學；電流

The interruption of electricity caused a great loss to our company.

電力的中斷使我們公司損失慘重。

6 **wire**   [waɪr]   *n.*   （金屬）線；電線

My wire is busy.

我電話忙線中。

electricity wires 電線

electrical wiring 電線線路

7 **shock**   [ʃɑk]   *n.*   衝擊；震驚   *vi.*   震動

His death was a great shock to us all.

他的死使我們大家都大為震驚。

8 **cab**   [kæb]   *n.*   計程車，出租單馬車

The secretary took a cab to her office.

那秘書搭計程車去她的辦公室。

9 **smoke**   [smok]   *n.*   煙；抽煙   *vi.*   冒煙

I can't stand the smell of tobacco. So stop smoking in front of me.

我受不了菸味，所以請別在我面前抽菸。

stop smoking 戒煙

have a smoke 抽根煙

10 wait　　[wet]　*vi.*　等，等候　*n.*　等待

We're waiting for the bus.

我們在等公車。

long wait 漫長的等待

keep someone waiting 讓某人等待

11 meter　　[`mitɚ]　*n.*　計量器，計，表

The meter reads 100.

儀表的讀數是 100。

12 fare　　[fɛr]　*n.*　車費，船費，票價

The bus fare is going to go up next month.

公車費下個月要上漲。

13 mechanic　　[mə`kænɪk]　*n.*　技工，機械，機修工

He has been a mechanic since he graduated from high school.

他從高中畢業後，就當技工。

14 garage　　[gə`rɑʒ]　*n.*　汽車間（或庫）

He worked in a garage as a mechanic.

他在汽車修理廠當技工。

15 mechanical　　[mə`kænɪk!]　*adj.*　機械的；力學的

He is a mechanical genius.

他是一個機械天才。

16 fix   [fɪks]   *vt.*   使固定；決定

Let's fix a date to meet.

我們來決定見面的日期。

fix a date for 確定……日期

fix up 整（修）理，安頓，固定起來，裝上

17 broken   [`brokən]   *adj.*   被打碎的，骨折的

Her heart is broken.

她的心碎了。

18 engine   [`ɛndʒən]   *n.*   發動機，引擎；機車

Those are the components of an engine.

那些是發動機的部件。

19 analyze   [`æn!ˌaɪz]   *vt.*   分析，分解

Can you analyze the structure of the sentence for me?

你能給我分析一下這個句子的結構嗎？

20 straighten   [`stretn]   *vt.*   把……弄直   *vi.*   挺起來

My dad straightened up the garage.

我爸爸整理了車庫。

21 wrench   [rɛntʃ]   *vt.*   擰，扭傷   *n.*   擰

My cousin closed the door so hard that he wrenched the handle off.

我表弟關門用力過猛，連門把手都擰了下來。

22 **tool**　[tul]　*n.*　工具；用具

He cannot find his metal tools.
他找不到他的金屬工具。
A carpenter's tools include saws, hammers and so on.
木匠的工具包括鋸、錘子等。
Advertising is a powerful tool.
廣告是很強大的工具。

23 **dig**　[dɪg]　*vt.*　掘，挖；採掘

The dog dug out a bone.
這隻狗挖出一根骨頭。
dig the ground 掘地
dig out 發掘出來

24 **concrete**　[`kɑnkrit]　*n.*　混凝土；具體物

These buildings are made of concrete and steel.
這些房屋是用鋼和混凝土建成的。
【同】specific, material
【反】abstract

25 **pour**　[por]　*vt.*　灌，倒　*vi.*　傾瀉

She poured herself another cup of tea.
她為自己又倒了一杯茶。
pour sth. in 把某東西注進……裡
pour…into… 注……進到……裡面

26 hammer [ˋhæmɚ] *n.* 錘，榔頭 *vt.* 錘擊

Hammer the nails into the door.
把釘子釘在門上。
hit the drum with hammers 用錘擊鼓

27 factory [ˋfæktərɪ] *n.* 工廠，製造廠

The company closed the factory because of a food safety scandal.
這家公司因為食安問題，關閉了工廠。
in the factory 在工廠裡
a paper making factory 一家造紙廠

28 worker [ˋwɝkɚ] *n.* 工人

How many workers do you have in your farm?
你的農場有幾個工人？
The workers are just coming out of the factory.
工人們正從工廠裡出來。
become a worker 成為一個工人

29 weaver [ˋwivɚ] *n.* 紡織工，編織者

His sister is a weaver in this factory.
他姐姐是這個工廠的一名紡織工。

30 baker [ˋbekɚ] *n.* 麵包師

This baker's bread is famous and popular.
這個麵包師的麵包既知名又受歡迎。

Government 政府

Track 06

1　leader　[`lidɚ]　*n.*　領袖；領導人

Who is your leader?

你們的領袖是誰？

2　president　[`prɛzədənt]　*n.*　總統

The president is supported by his citizens.

總統受人民支持。

3　govern　[`gʌvɚn]　*vt.*　統治，治理；支配

Do not try to govern others' opinions.

別試著去支配別人的意見。

4　lead　[lid]　*vt.*　領導

He will lead the discussion.

他會帶領大家討論。

lead a march 領導一個遊行

lead one's struggle for equal rights

領導爭取平等權利鬥爭

5 battle [ˋbætl̩] *vi.* 戰鬥 *vt.* 與……作戰

The soldiers battle with the enemy.

士兵們與敵人戰鬥。

in battle 在戰鬥中

lose the battle 戰敗

主題 1

6 minister [ˋmɪnɪstɚ] *n.* 大臣；部長

The minister declares his resignation unexpectedly.

該大臣無預警地宣布辭職。

the Minister of Justice 司法部長

the American minister 美國公使

7 prime [praɪm] *adj.* 首要的；基本的

She makes it her prime care.

她極為重視這件事。

8 senator [ˋsɛnətɚ] *n.* 參議員；評議員

We are very privileged to have Senator King with us this evening.

今晚有金參議員光臨，我們感到十分榮幸。

9 congress [ˋkɑŋgrəs] *n.* 大會；國會，議會

He introduced a motion to the Congress.

他向國會提交了一份議案。

10 **assembly**　[əˋsɛmblɪ]　*n.*　集合；集會；裝配

It's an unlawful assembly.

那是非法集會。

11 **deceitful**　[dɪˋsitfəl]　*adj.*　欺詐的

I advise you not to cooperate with that deceitful businessman.

我建議你不要和那個不誠實的商人合作。

12 **representative**　[ˏrɛprɪˋzɛntətɪv]　*adj.*　代表性的　*n.* 代表

He is a representative of the party.

他是政黨的代表。

13 **public**　[ˋpʌblɪk]　*adj.*　公共的，公眾的

We decided to make our views public.

我們決定把自己的觀點公開。

speak in public 在公眾面前講話

talk in public about this matter 在公眾面前談論這事

14 **servant**　[ˋsɝvənt]　*n.*　僕人，傭人

That lady cannot dispense with a servant.

那名貴婦不能沒有傭人。

15 vague　[veg]　*adj.*　模糊的，含糊的

We should not make vague promises.

我們不該作含糊不清的承諾。

【同】obscure, ambiguous

16 council　[ˋkaʊns!]　*n.*　理事會，委員會

We should submit our plans to the council for approval.

我們應該向理事會提交計畫以求批准。

17 local　[ˋlok!]　*adj.*　地方的；局部的

Have you read the local news this morning?

你今天早上看地方新聞了嗎？

18 county　[ˋkaʊntɪ]　*n.*　英國的郡，美國的縣

The county town is a hundred miles or so away from here.

縣城離這裡非常遠。

19 state　[stet]　*n.*　州；國家；政府

All the land belongs to the state in this country.

在這個國家土地全屬國有。

the United States 美國

in a poor state 狀況很糟

20 territory　[ˋtɛrə,torɪ]　*n.*　領土，版圖；領域

The war was carried into the territory of Southern Europe.

戰爭已伸展到南歐的領土。

21 **citizen** [ˋsɪtəzn] *n.* 公民；市民，居民

She is a lawful citizen.
她是個守法的公民。
American citizens 美國的公民
Citizen Rights Act 民權法案

22 **vote** [vot] *n.* 選舉，投票，表決

A large vote was polled.
投票踴躍。

23 **tax** [tæks] *vt.* 抽稅　*n.* 稅

The car is taxed until July.
這輛汽車七月前已上稅。
pay taxes 付稅
income tax 所得稅

24 **earn** [ɝn] *vt.* 賺得，掙得；獲得

He has earned a lot of money this month.
這個月他已經賺了好多錢了。
earn one's living by doing sth. 靠做某事謀生
earn a living as a painter 做畫家謀生

25 **police** [pəˋlis] *n.* 員警；員警當局

The police recovered the stolen jewelry.

警察找回了被盜的珠寶。

26 enforce [ɪn`fors] *vt.* 實施，執行；強制

Don't enforce your will on me, please.

請別把你的意願強迫在我身上。

【同】compel, oblige

27 arrest [ə`rɛst] *vt.* 逮捕，拘留；阻止

The police made several arrests.

員警逮捕了好幾個人。

28 fireman [`faɪrmən] *n.* 消防隊員

A brave fireman rescued the woman.

一個勇敢的消防隊員救了這女人。

29 protect [prə`tɛkt] *vt.* 保護

Having sunscreen can protect your skin from the sun.

抹防曬乳可以保護妳的皮膚受日曬。

protect…from… 阻止……

protect against 防止……侵襲

30 help [hɛlp] *v.* 幫忙

Help yourself.

別客氣。

help... out 幫（某人）解決困難，難題

help… with 幫某人做某事

主題 1

Department 部門

Track 07

1 **corporation** [ˌkɔrpəˈreʃən] *n.* 公司，企業；社團

It is a larger corporation in Asia.

這是一家亞洲的大公司。

2 **mission** [ˈmɪʃən] *n.* 使命，任務；使團

Jerry went on a secret mission, and he didn't let his family know.

Jerry 執行一項秘密使命，而且他沒有讓家人知道。

3 **national** [ˈnæʃənḷ] *adj.* 國家的；民族的

We are trying to sell the product to national and international markets.

我們正試著將產品賣到國內和國際的市場。

a national park 國家公園

【反】international

4 **branch** [bræntʃ] *n.* 枝條；支流；部門

The river has two main branches.

這條河有兩條主要的支流。

The company has branches all over the country.

該公司在全國各地均設有分公司。

a branch of the bank 支行
a party branch 黨支部

5 consist　　[kən`sɪst]　*vi.*　由 ... 組成；在於

The beauty of the building consists of its design and materials.
這座建築物的美在於它的設計與建材。
The committee consists of twenty members.
委員會由二十名成員組成。

6 office　　[`ɔfɪs]　*n.*　辦公室；處，局，社

She went to her office in a hurry.
她匆匆忙忙向電報局去了。
post office 郵局
teacher's office 教研室

7 department　　[dɪ`pɑrtmənt]　*n.*　部，司，局，處，系

He worked in the community welfare department.
他在社會福利部工作。
department store 百貨商店

8 assemble　　[ə`sɛmb!]　*vt.*　集合，召集；裝配

If the fire alarm goes off, staff should assemble outside the building.
火警警報響時全體人員應到樓外集合。

9 resource　　[rɪ`sors]　*n.*　資源

Resources management is an important business skill.

資源管理是一項重要的經營技能。

10 **export** 　[ɪks`port]　*vt.*　輸出，出口；運走

Prohibition was laid on the export of coal.

禁止煤輸出。

【反】import

11 **import** 　[`ɪmport]　*vt.*　*n.*　輸入，進口

There are too many incidental expenses when importing goods.

進口貨物的雜費太多了！

12 **plan** 　[plæn]　*n.*　*vt.*　計畫，打算

Do you have any interest in my plan?

你對我的計畫有任何興趣嗎？

plan a visit 計畫一次旅行

one's plan for the future 某人未來的計畫

13 **proceed** 　[prə`sid]　*vi.*　進行；繼續進行

The old lady paused to drink water and proceeded with her story.

老婦人停下來喝水，繼續講她的故事。

14 **arrange** 　[ə`rendʒ]　*vt.*　整理，分類，排列

It was arranged that she would leave the following summer.

已安排她於第二年夏天離開。

15 **develop** 　[dɪ`vɛləp]　*vt.*　使（顏色等）顯現

The printer developed the same fault again.

這台印表機又出現了同樣的毛病。

develop business 發展商業

16 solution [sə`luʃən] *n.* 解決，解答；溶解

They haven't found the solution yet, but I'm sure they're on the right track.

他們還沒有找到解決辦法，但我肯定他們的思路是對的。

17 procure [pro`kjʊr] *vt.* 獲得，取得，促成

The two companies procured a temporary agreement.

這兩家公司達成了臨時協議。

procure sth. for sb. 為某人獲得某物

18 material [mə`tɪrɪəl] *n.* 原料；材料

We need more materials to build the house.

我們需要更多原料來建房子。

What kind of materials will you need?

你需要甚麼材料？

19 production [prə`dʌkʃən] *n.* 生產；產品；總產量

We must increase production levels.

我們必須提高生產水準。

What kinds of materials will you need?

你需要甚麼樣的材料？

20 product [`prɑdəkt] *n.* 產品，產物；（乘）積

We try to figure out the new marketing policy for promoting our products.

我們試著想出新的行銷手法,來刺激我們的產品銷售。

milk product 奶類製品

21 **merchandise** [ˋmɝtʃənˌdaɪz] *n.* 商品,貨物

Their merchandise is of high quality.

他們的貨物品質很好。

They exhibit lots of foreign merchandise.

他們展示許多種外國商品。

22 **attribute** [əˋtrɪbjʊt] *vt.* 把……歸因於 *n.* 屬性

She attributes her success to her teacher's encouragement.

她把成功歸因於老師的鼓勵。

【同】ascribe

23 **promote** [prəˋmot] *vt.* 促進,發揚;提升

We must promote commerce with neighboring countries.

我們必須促進與鄰國的貿易。

【同】encourage

24 **advertise** [ˋædvɚˌtaɪz] *vt.* 通知 *vi.* 登廣告

We decided to advertise our new product.

我們決定為我們的新產品做廣告。

advertise sth. on TV / in a newspaper 在電視上或報紙做廣告

25 **commercial** [kəˋmɝʃəl] *adj.* 商業的;商品化的

Commercial television is an effective medium for advertising.
商業電視是有效的廣告宣傳工具。

26 sell [sɛl] *vt. vi.* 賣

主題 1

Do you sell stamps?
你們出售郵票嗎？

27 consumption [kənˋsʌmpʃən] *n.* 消費（量）；滅絕

The food is for their consumption on the trip to London.
這食物供他們去倫敦旅途中吃。

【同】expenditure, expense

【反】production

28 calculate [ˋkælkjə,let] *vt.* 計算；估計；計畫

My mom calculated the costs very carefully.
我媽媽仔細計算開支。

【同】count, compute

29 quality [ˋkwɑlətɪ] *n.* 品質

We should improve what is called the quality of living.
我們應該提高所謂的生活品質。

high quality 高品質
poor quality 劣質的

30 assurance [əˋʃʊrəns] *n.* 保證；財產轉讓書

He gave me his assurance that he would pay the bill.
他跟我保證他會付帳單。

Finance 金融

Track 08

1 trade [tred] *vi.* 經商,進行貿易

Japan does lots of trade with the United States.

日本與美國間的貿易頻繁。

trade with 與……交換（貿易）

The World Trade Center 世界貿易中心

2 exchange [ɪks`tʃendʒ] *vt.* 交換；交流 *n.* 交換

We exchange our opinions about the issue at the party.

在派對上,我們對這個議題交換了意見。

3 commodity [kə`mɑdətɪ] *n.* 日用品,商品,物品

May is the season for this commodity on our market.

五月份是這種商品在我方市場上銷售的季節。

【同】goods, merchandise

4 bond [bɑnd] *n.* 聯結,聯繫；公債

People were eager to buy government bonds in the past six months.

過去六個月人們急於購買政府公債。

His former employer bonded him, so he appreciated his kindness.

他前任老闆為他做保，因此他很感激他幫助。

主題 1

5 trader　　[`tredɚ]　*n.*　商人；商船

The trader is notable for his honesty.

這個商人以他的誠實出名。

6 increase　　[ɪn`kris]　*vt.*　*vi.*　*n.*　增加

There was a steady increase in population.

人口在不斷增長中。

increase to 增長到

be increased by 通過……來增加

7 bubble　　[`bʌb!]　*n.*　泡　*vi.*　冒泡，沸騰

The child is blowing bubbles in the yard.

那小孩在庭院裡吹泡泡。

bubble gum 泡泡糖

bubble bath 泡泡浴

8 scheme　　[skim]　*vt.*　計畫　*vi.*　搞陰謀

Your scheme is not practicable at all.

你的計劃一點都不可行。

【同】program, schedule, plan

9 income　　[`ɪn,kʌm]　*n.*　收入；收益；進款

Her income is well below the average.

她的收入大大低於平均水準。

【同】revenue, returns, gains

10 **amount**　[ə`maʊnt]　*n.*　總數；數量；和

The amount of cash is very large.

現金的總數很大。

【同】sum, total, quantity

11 **equivalent**　[ɪ`kwɪvələnt]　*adj.*　相等的；等量的

A dime is equivalent to ten pennies.

一角等於十分。

【同】same, equal, identical

【反】different

12 **order**　[`ɔrdɚ]　*n.*　訂貨；訂貨單

The company received a large order for computers.

這家公司接到一份要求大量供應電腦的訂單。

obey one's order 服從某人的命令

be arranged in order of size 按大小順序排列

13 **conjecture**　[kən`dʒɛktʃɚ]　*n.*　*v.*　推測，臆測

The president conjectured that his policy would do well.

總裁猜測他的策略會成功。

【同】speculation, supposition

【反】fact, reality

14 **dividend**　[`dɪvə,dɛnd]　*n.*　（股份的）紅利

The company declared a large dividend at the end of the year.

公司在年底宣佈紅利甚豐。

15 **recompense** [ˋrɛkəmˏpɛns] *v.* 報酬，賠償

The insurance company will recompense his loss.
保險公司賠償她的損失。

16 **allowance** [əˋlaʊəns] *n.* 津貼，補助費

They are indifferent to their retirement allowance.
他們對自己的養老金問題漠不關心。

17 **savings** [ˋsevɪŋz] *n.* 儲金

His parents spent almost all their savings to pay his tuition fees.
他的父母幾乎花光他們的積蓄，以支付他的學費。

18 **account** [əˋkaʊnt] *n.* 記述；解釋；帳目

I forget my account number.
我忘記我的帳號了。

19 **statement** [ˋstetmənt] *n.* 陳述，聲明

The purport of the statement is that the singer is going to retire.
該項聲明大意是說該歌手要退出演藝圈了。
【同】account, report, bulletin

20 **investment** [ɪnˋvɛstmənt] *n.* 投資，投資額，投入

She made an investment in real estate.
她投資了房地產。

21 loan　[lon]　*n.*　貸款；暫借　*vt.*　借出

How much interest do they charge on loans?

他們貸款收多少利息？

【同】lend, lease

【反】borrow

22 growth　[groθ]　*n.*　增長；增長量；生長

The rate of overall industrial growth was above ten percent.

工業總增長率超過百分之十。

23 risk　[rɪsk]　*n.*　風險，危險，冒險

He saved her life at the risk of his own.

他冒著自己的生命危險救了她的命。

【同】danger, peril, jeopardy

【反】safety

24 reward　[rɪˋwɔrd]　*n.*　報答；報酬　*vt.*　獎賞

You have received a just reward.

你已得到了應有的報酬。

Employees who pass the exam will be rewarded a bonus.

通過測驗的員工將可獲得獎金。

25 property　[ˋprɑpɚtɪ]　*n.*　財產；財產權

The old man has several properties in the country.

這個老人在鄉下有幾筆地產。

intellectual property 智慧財產權

26 plateau　　[plæ`to]　*n.*　高原；平穩時期

Our plan has reached to the plateau of development.

我們的計畫已經發展到了較高的水準。

27 price　　[praɪs]　*n.*　價格；代價

Prices keep going up.

物價持續上漲。

bring down the price 降價

a price list 價格表

當用 price 這個字，價格高、低會用 high / low 來表示，不是用

expensive / cheap。

28 distribution　　[ˌdɪstrə`bjuʃən]　*n.*　分發，分配；分布

Ian and his partners could not agree on the distribution of

the profits.

Ian 和他的夥伴對於利潤的分配意見不一致。

29 margin　　[`mardʒɪn]　*n.*　頁邊的空白；欄外

I made some notes in the margin when I was a student.

他在頁邊空白處做筆記。

30 balance　　[`bæləns]　*n.*　平衡；結餘

The girl lost her balance and fell over.

女孩身體失去平衡，摔了一跤。

The balance on your account is NT$ 120,000.

你的帳戶上結餘有新台幣十二萬元。

Organization 組織

 Track 09

1 executive [ɪgˋzɛkjʊtɪv] *n.* 總經理，董事

His nomination as chief executive was approved by the board.
他被提名為行政總裁的事被董事會批准了。

2 boss [bɔs] *n.* 老闆 *vt.* 指揮

He was fired by his boss last month.
他被他的老闆解雇了。

This is my boss, Mr. Thomson.
這位是我的老闆，湯姆遜先生。

3 dictate [ˋdɪktet] *vt.* *vi.* 口授；命令

Ted dictates letters to his secretary.
Ted 對他的秘書口授了一封信。

What right do you have to dictate me?
你有什麼權利命令我？

4 authorize [ˋɔθə͵raɪz] *v.* 授權，批准

She has been authorized to repossess inheritance.
她已經得到認可，重新擁有這筆遺產。

5 create [krɪˋet] *vt.* 創造；引起，產生

Some people believe that God created the world.

有些人相信上帝創造了世界。

Our purpose is to create wealth.

我們的目的就是創造財富。

主題 1

6 advertisement [ˌædvəˈtaɪzmənt] *n.* 廣告；公告；登廣告

They put an advertisement in the newspaper to promote their new product.

他們在報紙上登廣告來推銷新產品。

7 newspaper [ˈnjuzˌpepɚ] *n.* 報紙

My grandfather always reads newspaper while having breakfast.

我爺爺總在吃早餐時看報紙。

an evening newspaper 晚報

newspaper reporter 新聞記者

8 mail [mel] *n.* 郵件；郵遞

Do I have any mail today?

今天有我的信嗎？

by mail 通過郵寄

mail a letter 郵信

9 lazy [ˈlezɪ] *adj.* 懶惰的

A lazy youth, a lousy age.

【諺】少壯不努力，老大徒悲傷。

lazy people 懶人

a lazy river 流動緩慢的河

10 **industrious** [ɪnˋdʌstrɪəs] *adj.* 勤勞的，勤奮的

I knew that Danny was an industrious man.

我知道丹尼是一個勤勞的人。

11 **focus** [ˋfokəs] *vi.* 聚焦，注視 *n.* 焦點

All eyes were focused on us.

大家的眼光都注意著我們。

【同】core, center

12 **duty** [ˋdjutɪ] *n.* 義務；責任

One of her duties is to sort the letters.

她的職責之一是將信件歸檔。

13 **labor** [ˋlebɚ] *n.* 勞動，工作

My boss is very satisfied with your labors.

我的老闆對你的工作很滿意。

14 **union** [ˋjunjən] *n.* 聯合；聯合會，團結

They decide to join the union.

他們決定加入工會。

labor union 工會

15 **employer** [ɪmˋplɔɪɚ] *n.* 雇傭者，雇主

Ms. Chen is a very good employer. She treats her

employees well.

陳小姐是位好雇主。她非常善待她的員工。

16 interview　　[ˋɪntɚˌvju]　*vt.*　採訪

I have already interviewed twenty people for the job.

為了這個職缺，我已面試過二十位了。

Sam feels excited that he has the chance to interview the director about his latest movie.

Sam 有機會去採訪導演最新的電影，對此他感到很興奮。

17 reject　　[rɪˋdʒɛkt]　*vt.*　拋棄；拒收

Our proposal has been rejected.

我們的提案已被拒絕了。

18 system　　[ˋsɪstəm]　*n.*　系統，體系；制度

Do you know how to log on to the system?

你知道怎麼登錄進入這個系統嗎？

19 regulation　　[ˌrɛgjəˋleʃən]　*n.*　規章，規則；調節

This regulation refers only to children.

這些規定僅適用於兒童。

If you break the regulations, you will be fined.

如果你違反規則將會被罰款。

20 effective　　[ɪˋfɛktɪv]　*adj.*　有效的；有影響的

Aspirin is a highly effective treatment.

阿斯匹靈是非常有效的治療方法。

They are trying to find the drugs that are effective against cancer.
他們努力尋找有效對抗癌症的藥。

21 **advantage** [əd`væntɪdʒ] *n.* 優點，優勢；好處

Mary has the advantage of a good education.
Mary 具備受過良好教育的優勢。

22 **inspect** [ɪn`spɛkt] *vt.* 檢查，審查；檢閱

They inspected the roof for leaks.
他們檢查了屋頂看看是否有漏隙。
【同】check, examine, scrutinize

23 **execute** [`ɛksɪ,kjut] *vt.* 將……處死；實施

We started to execute a plan to reduce fuel consumption.
我們開始實施減碳計畫。

24 **chief** [tʃif] *n.* 領袖 *adj.* 為首的

Ms. Chang is the chief financial officer of the company.
張小姐是這家公司的財務長。
the chief of a police station 員警（分）局長
a chief engineer 總工程師

25 **engineer** [,ɛndʒə`nɪr] *n.* 工程師，技師

He is struggling to be an engineer.
他努力成為一名工程師。
ABC Engineering Company ABC 工程公司

26 chart [tʃɑrt] *n.* 圖，圖表；海圖

The chart showed the loss of the company.

圖表顯示公司的虧損。

【同】diagram, table, graph

27 title [`taɪtl̩] *n.* 權力；標題

Does the old man have any title to his land?

這位老人有他土地的所有權嗎？

title page〔書籍的〕書名頁（印有書名、作者、出版者等）

28 company [`kʌmpənɪ] *n.* 公司

Sammy and his wife set up a company last month.

Sammy 和他的太太上個月成立一間新公司。

a publishing company 出版社

set up a company 建立一個公司

29 establish [ə`stæblɪʃ] *vt.* 建立，設立；確立

Our company was established in 2011.

我們的公司成立於 2011 年。

【同】set up, found

30 share [ʃɛr] *vt.* 分享 *n.* 一份

It's never mean to share your care for others.

永遠別吝於向他人分享你的關懷。

Unit
10

Stationery 文具

Track 10

1 pen [pɛn] *n.* 筆；鋼筆

My father gave me a pen when I got a full-time job.
當我找到全職工作時，我爸爸送給我一枝鋼筆。

pen friend / pen pal 筆友
pen name 筆名

2 ink [ɪŋk] *n.* 墨水，油墨

There's an ink stain on your shirt.
你的襯衫上有一個墨水斑。

He wrote a letter in black ink.
他用黑墨水寫字。

ink-bottle 墨水瓶

3 pencil [ˋpɛns!] *n.* 鉛筆

This picture is drawn with pencils.
這幅畫是用鉛筆畫的。

pencil box 鉛筆盒
a hair pen 毛筆

4 sharpen [ˋʃɑrpn] *vt.* 削尖，使敏銳

Sharpen all the pencils in your pencil box before the test.

考試前先將你鉛筆盒的鉛筆削尖。

5 **draw** [drɔ] *vt.* *vi.* 畫；拉；牽；引出

I am going to draw some money from the account.
我要提領一些存款。

draw a picture on the wall 在牆上畫一張畫

draw a deep breath 深深吸一口氣

6 **lend** [lɛnd] *vt.* 把……借給

Would you please lend me your eraser?
請把橡皮擦借給我用用好嗎？

7 **marker** [mɑrkɚ] *n.* 作記號的人，記分員，書籤，紀念碑

Paul put a marker where the ball had landed.
Paul 在球掉的地方做記號。

a boundary marker 界標

8 **paper** [ˋpepɚ] *vt.* 用紙包裝（或覆蓋）

The wall was papered in pink.
牆壁糊上粉紅色壁紙。

important papers 重要的文件

write a paper 寫論文

9 **size** [saɪz] *n.* 尺寸，大小

I don't know the exact size of the boxes.
我不知道這些箱子的確定尺寸。

10 copy　[`kɑpɪ]　*vt.*　抄寫　*n.*　副本

Do not copy anyone's idea, or you'll be kicked out of my course.

別抄襲任何人點子，不然你會被我踢出我的課程。

take a copy of the letter 抄這封信

ten copies of the book　10 冊書

11 amend　[ə`mɛnd]　*vt.*　修正，改善，改良

Please amend your paper immediately.

請馬上修正你的論文。

【同】revise, mend

【反】impair

12 clip　[klɪp]　*vt.*　夾住　*n.*　夾子，鉗子

She asked her assistant to fasten the receipts with a paper clip.

她要她的助理用迴紋針將這些收據夾住。

13 photograph　[`fotə,græf]　*n.*　照片，相片

She planned to enlarge this photograph.

她計畫放大這張照片。

take a photograph of sb. / sth.

拍某人或某物的照片

14 file　[faɪl]　*n.*　檔案　*vt.*　把……歸檔

Please file those letters and the documents immediately.

請把這些信件存檔。

15 **multiply**   [ˋmʌltəplaɪ]   *vt.*   使增加；乘

Five multiplied by nine is forty-five.

九乘以五得四十五。

16 **divide**   [dəˋvaɪd]   *vt.*   分；分配；分開

The cake was divided into two pieces.

蛋糕被分成兩半。

divide into 把……分成

divide up 分配

17 **magnet**   [ˋmægnɪt]   *n.*   有吸引力的人（或物）；磁鐵

Sue collects many cute magnets.

Sue 蒐集很多可愛的磁鐵。

Here are some magnets. Do you need some?

這裡有一些磁鐵。你需要嗎？

18 **rubber**   [ˋrʌbɚ]   *n.*   橡皮

Rubber is elastic.

橡皮是有彈性的。

Did you see my rubber?

你有看到我的橡皮擦嗎？

a rubber band 橡皮帶

19 **folder**   [ˋfoldɚ]   *n.*   文件夾

Could you buy some folders on your way to the post office?

你去郵局的途中可以買些文件夾嗎？

20 **wrap**　[ræp]　*vt.*　裹，包，捆

She wrapped the book carefully.

她小心翼翼地包書。

21 **note**　[not]　*n.*　鈔票，紙幣；筆記

There is a note on my desk.

我桌上有張紙條。

take notes 作筆記

make a note 做記錄

22 **extract**　[ɪk`strækt]　*vt.*　取出；榨取　*n.*　摘錄

Mom extracted a small notebook from her handbag.

媽媽從手提包裡取出了一個小筆記本。

【同】obtain, remove

【反】insert

23 **pad**　[pæd]　*n.*　墊；本子　*vt.*　填塞

Remember to put a clean pad of cotton over your wound.

記得在你的傷口上敷一塊乾淨的紗布墊。

mouse pad = mouse mat 滑鼠墊

24 **shelf**　[ʃɛlf]　*n.*　擱板，架子

The dictionary is on the topmost shelf.

字典在最高的架子上。

【同】ledge, mantelpiece, step

25 **envelope**　[`ɛnvə,lop]　*n.*　信封

She put a card in the envelope.
她在信封裡放了一張卡片。
first day envelope 首日封
stamped addressed envelope
預先寫好姓名地址並貼上郵票的回信信封

26 label   [`leb!]   *n.*   標籤；標記，符號
I ask my employees to stick labels on the goods.
我要求我的員工在商品上貼標籤。
【同】tag, ticket

27 seal   [sil]   *n.*   封蠟；印記   *vt.*   封
Seal the envelope firmly.
將信封牢牢地密封起來。

28 tuck   [tʌk]   *vt.*   折短，卷起；塞
He tucked the letter into an envelope.
他把信折好塞進信封。

29 calendar   [`kæləndɚ]   *n.*   日曆，曆書；曆法
I put the calendar on the desk.
我把桌曆放在書桌上。

30 function   [`fʌŋkʃən]   *n.*   功能；職務；函數
Could you explain the function of the machine for me?
你能幫我解釋這台機器的功能嗎？

Unit
11

Equipment 設備

🔘 *Track 11*

1 equipment [ɪˋkwɪpmənt] *n.* 裝備；設備
He tried to fix the equipment, but he failed.
他想把機器修理好，但是失敗了

2 typewriter [ˋtaɪp,raɪtɚ] *n.* 打字機
Could you lend me your typewriter?
你可以借我打字機嗎？

3 electric [ɪˋlɛktrɪk] *adj.* 電的，電動的
The child likes electric toys.
這孩子喜歡電動玩具。
electric train 電動火車
an electric light 電燈

4 computer [kəmˋpjutɚ] *n.* 電腦，電腦
I got a new computer for a birthday present.
我得到一台電腦作生日禮物。
computer science 電腦科學
be kept on the computer 保存在電腦裡

5 importance [ɪm`pɔrtns] *n.* 重要；重要性

She emphasized the importance of careful driving.
她強調小心駕駛的重要性。

People recognize the importance of the computer.
人們認識到電腦的重要性。

be of importance = be important 重要的

6 machinery [mə`ʃɪnərɪ] n.（總稱）機器；機構

Many products are made by machinery right now.
現在有很多產品都是機器製造的了。

7 inform [ɪn`fɔrm] *vt.* 通知，向……報告

Please inform me once you receive my application.
如果你收到我的申請，請你告知我。

8 facility [fə`sɪlətɪ] *n.* 設備；容易；便利

We had no cooking facilities in our suite.
我們套房裡沒有烹飪設備。

【同】device, equipment

9 modern [`mɑdən] *adj.* 現代的

Women can speak out about politics in modern times.
現代女人可以公開談論政治。

in modern times 在現在時代

modern gymnastics 現代體育

10 **machine** [məˋʃin] *n.* 機器；機械

This machine is waterproof.

這台機器防水。

a washing machine 洗衣機

answer machine 留言機

11 **outlet** [ˋaʊtˏlɛt] *n.* 電源插座

Plug the lamp into the outlet.

把檯燈插頭插進電源插座裡。

12 **fan** [fæn] *n.* 電扇；扇子

My sister cooled herself with a fan.

我妹妹用扇子納涼。

an electric fan 電扇

a football fan 足球迷

13 **desk** [dɛsk] *n.* 書桌，辦公桌

There are three books on the desk.

書桌上有三本書。

on the desk 在書桌上

work at one's desk 在桌子上工作

14 **demonstrate** [ˋdɛmənˏstret] *vt.* 說明；論證；表露

Please demonstrate how the machine works.

請示範這台機器的使用方法。

15 automatic [ˌɔtə`mætɪk] *adj.* 自動的；機械的

This washing machine is fully automatic.

這台洗衣機是全自動的。

semi-automatic *adj.* 半自動的

16 repair [rɪ`pɛr] *vt.* *n.* 修理，修補

He turned the chair on its side to repair it.

他把椅子翻轉過來修理。

be under repair 正在修理

17 measure [`mɛʒɚ] *vt.* 量，測量 *n.* 分量

They measured the length of the room.

他們量了房間的長度。

18 print [prɪnt] *vt.* *n.* 印刷

The print is too small for my grandpa to read.

印刷字體太小，我爺爺看不清。

be printed out 被列印出來

fast-moving printing machine 快速印刷機

19 supply [sə`plaɪ] *vt.* *n.* 供給，供應

Demand began to exceed supply.

開始供不應求。

supply the energy for sth. 為某東西提供能源

Office Supplies Company 辦公用品公司

20 cabinet [ˋkæbənɪt] *n.* 櫥，櫃；內閣

The Cabinet meets regularly.

內閣定期開會。

Cabinet reshuffle 內閣改組

21 replace [rɪˋples] *vt.* 把⋯放回；取代

He replaced the book on the shelf.

她把書放回到書架上。

22 downward [ˋdaʊnwəd] *adv.* 向下；⋯⋯以下

The officer looked downward to avoid the woman's eyes.

軍官低著頭看，以避開婦女的目光。

23 rise [raɪz] *vi.* 起立；升起；上漲

The sun rises in the east and sets in the west.

太陽從東方升起，在西方落下。

rise to 增長到

rise from sw.

從某地方升（站）起來

24 illuminate [ɪˋlumə͵net] *vt.* 照明，照亮；闡明

A smile illuminated my mother's face.

微笑使我的媽媽容光煥發。

【同】enlighten, illustrate

25 sign [saɪn] *n.* 招牌；徵兆，跡象，病症

Stock prices are showing signs of revival.

股價有復甦的徵兆。

26 pack　[pæk]　*vt.*　捆紮；擠滿　*n.*　包

The bus was packed with noisy children.

這輛公共汽車裡擠滿了吵吵嚷嚷的小孩。

a packing case 包裝箱

pack sth. up 把某東西打包

27 casement　[`kesmənt]　*n.*　窗

There are two casements in this house.

這間屋子有兩扇窗戶。

28 sturdy　[`stɝdɪ]　*adj.*　堅定的；牢固的

Fences must be sturdy.

圍籬必須是牢固耐用的。

【同】lusty, strong , stout, firm

【反】frail, weak, flimsy

29 cart　[kɑrt]　*n.*　手推車；二輪運貨馬車

People in the 18th century delivered goods by cart.

18 世紀的人們用馬車送貨。

a two-wheeled cart pulled by a bare-footed man

一個兩輪的赤腳的人拉的馬。

30 lorry　[`lɔrɪ]　*n.*　運貨汽車，卡車

The boxes fell off the back of that lorry.

箱子從卡車後面掉下來。

Unit
12

Office Politics 辦公室政治

Track 12

1 **politic** [`pɑlə,tɪk] *adj.* 精明的，圓滑的，慎重的，策略的

A politic man tries not to offend people.

精明的人儘量不得罪人。

2 **senior** [`sinjɚ] *adj.* 年少的；地位較高的

She was unfit for such a senior position.

她不能勝任這樣的高級職位。

3 **member** [`mɛmbɚ] *n.* 成員，會員

She is a member of the Royal College of Nursing.

她是皇家護士協會的會員。

founder member 創辦人；發起人

private member 下院議員

4 **position** [pə`zɪʃən] *n.* 主張，立場；工作；形勢

The bookstore used to be in this position.

書店過去在這個位置。

He holds a high position in the company.

他在公司裡有很高的職位。

He got a position in the company.

他在那個公司謀得一職。

5 **superior**　　[sə`pɪrɪə]　　*n.*　　上司，上級

She always does what her superiors tell her.

她唯上級之命是從。

6 **inferior**　　[ɪn`fɪrɪə]　　*n.*　　下級；晚輩，次品

She is kind to her inferiors.

她對晚輩很親切。

【同】lower, subsidiary, poor

【反】superior

7 **behavior**　　[bɪ`hevjə]　　*n.*　　行為，舉止，態度

Her behavior showed she was an evil person.

她的行為表明她是一個邪惡的人。

influence someone's behavior 影響某人的行為

good / bad behavior 好行為／壞行為

8 **gossip**　　[`gɑsəp]　　*n.*　　閒談；碎嘴子；漫筆

I am busy right now, so I can't stay gossiping with you.

我現在很忙，不能和你閒聊了。

9 **aim**　　[em]　　*n.*　　瞄準；目標；目的

He aimed at the target but hit the wall.

他瞄準了目標射擊，但卻打在了牆上。

What was your aim in life?

你的生活目的是什麼？

aim at doing sth. 目的是在於做某事

10 listen [ˋlɪsn] *vi.* 聽，留神聽；聽從

She is listening to the radio.

她在聽收音機。

listen to the songs 聽歌曲

listen to sb. 聽某人說話

11 conflict [ˋkɑnflɪkt] *n.* 爭論；衝突；鬥爭

There is a conflict between these two tribes.

這兩個部落有衝突。

12 challenge [ˋtʃælɪndʒ] *n.* 挑戰；要求，需要

This career offers a challenge.

這份職業具有挑戰性。

13 answer [ˋænsɚ] *vt.* 回答；回應；適應

He has had no answer to his letter.

他的信沒收到回信。

answer the phone 回電話

14 caution [ˋkɔʃən] *n.* 小心；告誡 *vt.* 警告

Be aware of the caution.

小心警告。

15 reputation [ˌrɛpjəˋteʃən] *n.* 名譽，名聲；好名聲

She spotted her reputation by lying repeatedly.

她因反覆說謊而敗壞了自己的名聲。

16 question　[`kwɛstʃən]　*n.*　發問；問題；疑問

There's no question about his honesty.

他無疑是誠實的。

out of question 毫無疑問

out of the question 不可能

17 complain　[kəm`plen]　*vi.*　抱怨，訴苦；控告

I'm tired of complaining about my life.

我厭倦抱怨我的生活了。

18 struggle　[`strʌg!]　*n.*　*vi.*　鬥爭，奮鬥

We all struggle for making a living.

我們都在努力維生。

struggle against 與……做鬥爭（搏鬥），打仗

struggle for 為……而鬥爭

19 satisfy　[`sætɪs,faɪ]　*vt.*　使滿意；使滿足

She never satisfies her curiosity.

她永遠無法滿足她的好奇心。

That answer won't satisfy them.

那個答案不能使他們感到滿意。

20 promotion　[prə`moʃən]　*n.*　促進；提升；創立

There are good chances of promotion in this firm.

這家公司裡提升的機會很多。

21 raise [rez] *vt.* 提出，發起，發出

None of them raised any objection.

他們誰也沒提出反對意見。

The weight is too heavy; I can't raise it.

重量太重，我不能舉起它。

22 opinion [ə`pɪnjən] *n.* 意見，看法，主張

In my opinion, I don't think you must accept his apology.

就我的看法，我不認為你一定得接受他的道歉。

give one's opinion 表達某人的看法

23 affirm [ə`fɝm] *vt.* 斷言，批准；證實

I affirm that what he said is true.

我斷言他所說的是實情。

24 introduce [ˌɪntrə`djus] *vt.* 提出（議案等）

The chairman introduced a topic for discussion.

主席提出議題供大家討論。

ask to be introduced to sb. 請求被介紹給某人

be introduced to sb. as ... 作為⋯⋯介紹給某人

25 romance [ro`mæns] *n.* 傳奇；浪漫文學

She liked to read romances.

她喜歡讀浪漫故事。

【同】love affair, relationship

主題 1

26 **allow** [əˋlaʊ] *vt.* 允許，准許；任

She won't allow us to smoke.

她不允許我們抽煙。

allow sb. to do sth. 允許某人做某事

be allowed to change 允許改變（換）

27 **forbid** [fəˋbɪd] *vt.* 禁止；不許

Smoking is forbidden in this office.

這間辦公室禁止吸煙。

forbid sb. to do sth. 禁止某人做某事

be forbidden to do sth. 被禁止做某事

28 **obey** [əˋbe] *vt.* 順從 *vi.* 服從

You should obey your parents.

你應該順從你的父母。

tell sb. to obey 告訴某人聽話（服從）

29 **influence** [ˋɪnflʊəns] *n.* 勢力，權勢

The influence of global warming is obvious.

溫室效應的影響是明顯的。

30 **exploit** [ɪkˋsplɔɪt] *vt.* 剝削；利用；開拓

Mr. White opened a company to exploit the resources in that area.

懷特先生開立一間公司來充分利用那個區域的資源。

主題 2
Country & News
國家與新聞

Unit
01

System 制度

🔵 *Track 13*

1 system [ˋsɪstəm] *n.* 系統，體系；制度

Do you know how to log in to the system?

你知道怎麼登錄進入這個系統嗎？

2 government [ˋgʌvənmənt] *n.* 政府；治理；政治

He is a student of government.

他研究政治學。

hold important jobs in government 在政府裡有重要的工作（職位）

3 commonwealth [ˋkɑmən‚wɛlθ] *n.* 共和國；聯邦

The Commonwealth agreed to make a compact with this country.

英聯邦同意和這個國家訂約。

Common Wealth of Australia 澳大利亞聯邦（澳洲）

4 parliament [ˋpɑrləmənt] *n.* 議會，國會

Parliament won't be in session again until after New Year.

國會將等到新年後才再進入會期。

Houses of Parliament 英國國會大廈

parliamentary procedure 會議程序

5 capital [ˋkæpət!] *n.* 資本，資金；首都

Tokyo is the capital of Japan.

東京是日本的首都。

capital letters 大寫字母

the capital city 首都

6 alderman [ˋɔldəmən] *n.* 市府參事，市議員

The alderman was not respected by the citizens.

這位市議員並不受到市民的敬重。

7 represent [ˌrɛprɪˋzɛnt] *vt.* 描繪；代表；象徵

This picture represents a scene at King Lear's palace.

這幅畫描繪了李爾王宮庭的一個場面。

8 issue [ˋɪʃʊ] *n.* 問題；發行 *vt.* 發行

The politician is trying to keep a low profile on this issue.

政客力圖在這個問題上保持低姿態。

issue a passport / visa 核發護照／簽證

9 enact [ɪnˋækt] *v.* 制定（法律），扮演（角色）

Several bills were enacted at the end of this session of Parliament.

幾項法案在這屆國會的會議結束時被頒佈。

10 ordinance [ˋɔrdɪnəns] *n.* 法令，條

You should obey the government ordinance.

你必須遵守這條政府法令。

arbitration ordinance 仲裁法條

11 **royal**　[ˋrɔɪəl]　*adj.*　王的；皇家的

The royal family will pay a visit to the neighboring country this weekend.

王族家庭這週末將會拜訪鄰國。

royal highness 皇家親屬間的稱呼

12 **realm**　[rɛlm]　*n.*　王國，國土；領域

The diplomat made outstanding contributions in the realm of foreign affairs.

該名外交官在外交領域上作出了卓越貢獻。

a realm of imagination or fantasy 仙境，幻境想像或幻想的王國

13 **castle**　[ˋkæs!]　*n.*　城堡；巨大建築物

The spirit haunts the castle.

幽靈常出沒於這間城堡。

the Magic Castle 神秘城堡

the Sleeping Beauty Castle 睡美人城堡

Castle In The Sky 天空之城（宮崎駿動畫）

14 **palace**　[ˋpælɪs]　*n.*　宮，宮殿

The furniture of the palace was made of beaten gold.

宮殿的家具由金箔做成。

the Children's Palace 少年宮

the Worker's Palace of Culture 工人文化宮

15 queen　　[`kwin]　　*n.*　　女王；王后

She was the queen of society then.

那時她是社交界女王。

England has a queen now.

英國現在女王在位。

The king has a pretty queen.

年輕的國王有個美麗的王妃。

主題 **2**

16 velvet　　[`vɛlvɪt]　　*n.*　　絲絨，天鵝絨

The queen assumed a velvet dress.

王后穿了一件天鵝絨禮服。

17 confer　　[kən`fɚ]　　*vt.*　　授予

Queen Victoria conferred knighthood on several distinguished men.

維多利亞女王將爵士頭銜授予幾位傑出人士。

【同】grant, award, present

18 king　　[kɪŋ]　　*n.*　　國王，君主

The lion is called the king of beasts.

獅子號稱百獸之王。

19 judgment　　[`dʒʌdʒmənt]　　*n.*　　意見；審判；判斷

We are waiting for God's dreadful judgment.

我們在等待上帝令人生畏的審判。

judgment day 審判日

poor judgment 判斷失誤

20 liege [lidʒ] *n.* 君主，王侯，臣下

My liege!
君王陛下！
liege homage 宣誓效忠
liege men 臣民

21 prostrate [`prɑstret] *v.* 拜倒，使俯臥，使……屈服

They prostrated themselves before the queen.
他們拜倒在女王的腳下。

22 princess [`prɪnsɪs] *n.* 公主，王妃

The kind dwarves asked the princess to have dinner with them.
善良的小矮人們邀請公主和他們一起吃晚飯。

23 empress [`ɛmprɪs] *n.* 皇后，女皇帝

The empress asked her son to marry the princess of the neighboring kingdom.
皇后要求兒子娶鄰國的公主。
the Empress Dowager 皇太后
Empress Wu 武則天

24 emperor [`ɛmpərə] *n.* 皇帝

The emperor conferred a title on the soldier.
皇上授予這士兵一頭銜。
Japanese Emperor 日本天皇

25 formal [`fɔrml] *adj.* 正式的；禮儀上的

She was invited to a formal luncheon.
我們被邀參加一次正式的午宴。

26 **prince**　[prɪns]　*n.*　王子，親王

The old witch charmed the prince.
女巫對王子施了魔法。
prince charming 白馬王子／夢中情人
The Little Prince 小王子

27 **charity**　[ˋtʃærətɪ]　*n.*　施捨；慈善事業

This charity aimed to help people to help themselves.
這一慈善團體過去的宗旨是幫助人們實行自助。
charity ball 募款舞會

28 **sovereign**　[ˋsɑvrɪn]　*n.*　君主　*adj.*　統治的

A sultan is a sovereign ruler of certain Muslim countries.
蘇丹是某些穆斯林國家的最高統治者。
【同】ruling, royal, imperial

29 **monarch**　[ˋmɑnɚk]　*n.*　君主，最高統治者

The monarch is head of state.
君主是國家的元首。

30 **majesty**　[ˋmædʒɪstɪ]　*n.*　威嚴，尊嚴；陛下

The king was seated on the throne in all his majesty.
國王威嚴地坐在王座上。
Your majesty! 國王陛下！

主題 2

Unit
02

Military 軍隊

Track 14

1 military [ˋmɪlə͵tɛrɪ] *adj.* 軍事的；軍人的

There used to be a military base in the region.

這地區過去有個軍事基地。

military service 兵役

military camp 軍營

2 army [ˋɑrmɪ] *n.* 軍隊

Gibson is in the army.

Gibson 服務於陸軍。

serve in the army 服兵役

3 navy [ˋnevɪ] *n.* 海軍

They enlisted five hundred recruits for the navy.

他們為海軍招募了五百名新兵。

Our navy is made up of all our warships.

我們的海軍是由我們所有的戰艦組成。

4 soldier [ˋsoldʒɚ] *n.* 士兵，戰士

How long have you been a soldier?

你當了多長時間的兵了？

5 sailor [`selə] *n.* 水手，海員，水兵

My brother was a sailor, and I'm going to be one, too.

我哥哥以前是水手，而我也打算當水手。

The old sailor had worked on many ships.

那個老船員已在許多船上工作過。

6 rank [ræŋk] *n.* 排 *vi.* 列為；社會階層

This tennis player is ranked third in the world.

這位網球運動員排名世界第三。

rank and file 一般成員，一般大眾

主題 2

7 general [`dʒɛnərəl] *adj.* 總的；一般的 *n.* 將軍

Napoleon was a great general.

拿破崙是一位偉大的將領。

general idea 總的思想，概念

get a general idea 瞭解大意（基本思想）

8 officer [`ɔfəsə] *n.* 軍官

The officers lived here and the enlisted men over there.

軍官住在這裡，士兵住在那裡。

public officers 公務員

9 enlist [ɪn`lɪst] *v.* （使）入伍從軍，徵募

He enlisted when he was 19.

他 19 歲時入伍。

10 **rifle**　[`raɪf!]　*n.*　步槍，來福槍

Get a rifle that shoots straight.
找一支射得準的步槍來。

11 **bayonet**　[`beənɪt]　*n.*　（槍上的）刺刀

The soldier bayoneted his way out.
士兵們用刺刀殺出一條血路。

at the point of a bayonet 以武力脅迫

12 **prevent**　[prɪ`vɛnt]　*vt.*　預防，防止；阻止

Rubber seals were used to prevent the water rubes from leaking.
裝上橡皮栓以防止水管漏水。

Nothing can prevent her from singing.
沒什麼東西能阻止她唱歌。

prevent sb. from doing sth. 阻止某人做某事

13 **invasion**　[ɪn`veʒən]　*n.*　入侵，侵略；侵犯

The king is determined to resist invasion.
國王決定抵抗入侵。

invasion of privacy 侵犯隱私權
culture invasion 文化侵略

14 **campaign**　[kæm`pen]　*n.*　戰役；運動

He will act as spearhead of the campaign.
他將在這場運動中掛帥。

15 **defense**　[dɪˋfɛns]　*n.*　防衛，防衛物

The reason why the police shot was in pure self-defense.

開槍純粹是為了自衛。

defense attorney 辯護律師

16 **defend**　[dɪˋfɛnd]　*vt.*　保衛，防守

We shall defend our city, whatever the cost may be.

不管代價如何，我們要捍衛我們的城市。

We shall defend our motherland.

我們將保衛我們祖國。

17 **weapon**　[ˋwɛpən]　*n.*　武器，兵器

This weapon fires anti-aircraft missiles.

這種武器是發射防空導彈的。

chemical weapon 生化武器

18 **artillery**　[ɑrˋtɪlərɪ]　*n.*　大炮，炮兵

Artillery fire caused great damage.

重炮轟擊造成大損害。

artillery shells 生化武器

19 **ammunition**　[͵æmjəˋnɪʃən]　*n.*　軍火，彈藥

The soldiers expended all their ammunition in that fight.

士兵在那場戰鬥中用盡了所有的彈藥。

20 **gunpowder**　[ˋgʌn͵paʊdə]　*n.*　黑色火藥；有煙火藥

Gunpowder is an explosive.

火藥是一種爆炸物。

sit on a barrel of gunpowder 提心吊膽

Gunpowder Tea 珠茶（中國產）

21 **enemy** ［ˋɛnəmɪ］ *n.* 敵人；仇敵；敵兵

Don't make an enemy of her.

不要與她為敵。

22 **invade** ［ɪnˋved］ *vt.* 入侵，侵略；侵襲

The Normans invaded England in 1066.

諾曼人於 1066 年入侵英國。

【同】raid, occupy, encroach

23 **attack** ［əˋtæk］ *vt.* *vi.* *n.* 攻擊，進攻

The enemy attacked us at night.

敵人在夜裡向我們進攻。

heart attack 心臟病發作

under attack 受到攻擊（抨擊）、遭到破壞

24 **battle** ［ˋbæt!］ *vi.* 戰鬥 *vt.* 與……作戰

The sailors battle with the winds and waves.

水手們與風浪搏鬥。

in battle 在戰鬥中

25 **ship** ［ʃɪp］ *n.* 輪船

The ship was due to sail the following afternoon.

這艘船預定在第二天下午起航。

26 boat 　[bot]　*n.*　小船，艇；漁船

Don't miss the boat.

【諺】不要錯失良機。

take a boat for sw. 乘船去某地

go to sw. by boat 乘船去某地

27 harbor 　['hɑrbɚ]　*n.*　港，避難所　*v.*　包庇，隱匿

The bombers made a strike on the harbor.

轟炸機對這港口進行了一次襲擊。

natural harbor 天然港

28 wound 　[wund]　*n.*　創傷，傷　*vt.*　使受傷

The wound is healing fast.

傷口癒合得很快。

You should have washed the wound.

你應該清洗傷口。

have a head wound 頭受傷

29 capture 　['kæptʃɚ]　*vt.*　捕獲，俘獲；奪得

The police have not captured the robber yet.

警方還沒有捕獲那個強盜。

30 prisoner 　['prɪznɚ]　*n.*　囚犯

The prisoner escaped by digging an underground tunnel.

囚犯挖了一條地道逃跑了。

Money 錢

1 **cash**　[kæʃ]　*n.*　現金，現款

We give a 20 percent discount for cash.

現金付款，我們八折優惠。

cash card 提款卡

cash payment 付現

2 **coin**　[kɔɪn]　*n.*　硬幣；鑄造（硬幣）

She put a coin into the insertion slot.

她往投幣孔投入一枚硬幣。

collect rare coins 收集稀有硬幣

a broken coin 一枚破損的硬幣

3 **silver**　[`sɪlvə]　*n.*　銀；銀子；銀器

Every cloud has a silver lining.

【諺】黑暗中總有一絲光明。

4 **copper**　[`kɑpə]　*n.*　銅；銅幣，銅制器

Copper and gold are both metals.

銅和金都是金屬。

5　pound　[paʊnd]　*n.*　英鎊（英國貨幣單位），磅（重量單位）

This book costs 10 pounds.

這本書值 10 英鎊。

Two cupfuls of water weigh about a pound.

兩滿杯的水秤起來大約一磅。

6　dollar　[`dɑlɚ]　*n.*　美元（美國貨幣單位）

She gave each child a dollar apiece.

她給每個孩子每人一美元。

bet a dollar to a donut 對某事深信不疑

to feel like a million dollars 身體健康

主題 2

7　earn　[ɝn]　*vt.*　賺得，掙得；獲得

He has earned a lot of money this month.

這個月他已經賺了好多錢了。

earn one's living by doing sth. 靠做某事謀生

earn a living as a painter 做畫家謀生

8　worth　[wɝθ]　*adj.*　值得……的

The house is worth a lot of money.

這棟房子值很多錢。

9　value　[`vælju]　*vt.*　尊重，重視，評價

My father values honesty beyond all things.

我父親把誠實看得比什麼都重要。

not good value for money 花這錢不值

10 **doubtful**　[ˋdaʊtfəl]　*adj.*　難以預測的；懷疑的

The ethics of his decision are doubtful.

他的這一決定是否合乎道德規範值得懷疑。

11 **creditor**　[ˋkrɛdɪtɚ]　*n.*　債權人

The poor man ran away from his creditors.

這個窮人躲避他的債主。

12 **deposit**　[dɪˋpɑzɪt]　*vt.*　使沉澱；存放

He deposited 5,000 dollars in the bank.

他在銀行存了五千元。

to make a deposit 存款（銀行）

security deposit 押金

13 **withdraw**　[wɪðˋdrɔ]　*vt.*　收回；撤回　*vi.*　撤退

The troops are being gradually withdrawn.

部隊正被漸漸撤回。

to make a withdraw 提款（銀行）

to withdraw troops 撤兵

14 **check**　[tʃɛk]　*n.*　支票

She wrote her friend a check, but it bounced.

她開了一張支票給她的母親，但是支票被退票了。

check in 報到，簽到，住飯店登記

check out 查明，結帳，查出

15 **worry**　[`wɝɪ]　*vt.*　（使）擔憂

They worried over their father's health.

他們為父親的健康擔憂。

be worried about sth. (sb.) 擔心某事（某人）

worry about doing sth. 擔心做某事

16 **obtain**　[əb`ten]　*vt.*　獲得，得到，買到

The leech hangs around other people hoping to obtain money.

那個詐財者依附於他人希望獲得錢財。

17 **buy**　[baɪ]　*vt.*　買

Money can't buy happiness.

【諺】金錢買不來幸福。

buy sb. sth. 給某人買某東西

buy sth. for sb. 給某人買某東西

18 **evil**　[`ivl]　*adj.*　邪惡的　*n.*　罪惡

His evil designs were frustrated.

他的罪惡企圖未能得逞。

to return good for evil 以德報怨

19 **purchase**　[`pɝtʃəs]　*n.*　買，購買　*vt.*　買

You can rely on your solicitor's professionalism in dealing with the land purchase.

你盡可依靠律師處理購房事宜。

20 credit　[ˋkrɛdɪt]　*n.*　信用貸款；信用

Our international credit is excellent.

我們的國際信譽極好。

21 invest　[ɪnˋvɛst]　*vt.*　投資；投入

She invested heavily in the cotton business.

她在棉花生意上投入鉅資。

22 wealth　[wɛlθ]　*n.*　財富，財產；豐富

Success and wealth transformed her character.

成功和財富改變了她的性格。

They had only one objective—to gain wealth.

他們只有一個目標──贏得財產。

23 fortune　[ˋfɔrtʃən]　*n.*　命運，運氣；財產

Everyone is the architect of his own fortune.

【諺】每個人都是自己命運的創造者。

I've heard all about her good fortune.

我已聽說所有關於她的好運氣。

24 ambition　[æmˋbɪʃən]　*n.*　雄心，抱負，野心

A person with his ambition won't stay long in a potty little firm like this.

一個有雄心大志的人在這樣一個不起眼的小公司裡是待不久的。

25 boundless　[ˋbaʊndlɪs]　*adj.*　無限的，無邊無際

The masses have boundless creative power.

人民群眾有無限的創造力。

boundless love 無盡的愛

26 success [sək`sɛs] *n.* 成功，成就，勝利

Congratulations on your success!

祝賀你的成功！

The new play was a great success.

這個新劇很成功。

27 considerable [kən`sɪdərəb!] *adj.* 相當大的；重要的

Mr. Robinson is a considerable person in his town.

羅賓森先生是鎮上的一位重要人物。

28 millionaire [ˌmɪljən`ɛr] *n.* 百萬富翁

The guy spends as if he were a millionaire.

那個男人用起錢來像個百萬富翁似的。

an overnight millionaire 暴發戶

29 treasury [`trɛʒərɪ] *n.* 寶藏

This book is a treasury of useful information.

這本書是有價值的資訊寶庫。

treasury map 藏寶圖

Treasury Bond 國庫長期債卷（美）

30 bank [bæŋk] *n.* 銀行；庫；岩，堤

They stood on the river bank to fish.

他們站在河岸邊釣魚。

主題 2

Culture 文化

Track 16

1　culture　[ˋkʌltʃɚ]　*n.*　文化，文明；教養

Advancing culture is bound to triumph over declining culture.

先進的文化必然戰勝沒落的文化。

【同】civilization, customs

2　civilization　[ˌsɪvḷəˋzeʃən]　*n.*　文明，文化；開化

Egyptian civilization is one of the oldest in the world.

埃及文明是世上最古老的文明之一。

Chinese Civilization 中國文明

3　custom　[ˋkʌstəm]　*n.*　習慣，風俗；海關

Custom rules the law.

【諺】風俗左右法律。

follow local custom 按照本地的習慣

give up one's own customs and way of life 放棄自己的習慣和生活方式

4　mutual　[ˋmjutʃʊəl]　*adj.*　相互的；共同的

We have many mutual friends on Facebook.

我們在臉書上有很多共同好友。

Mutual Interest 共同利益

5 communion [kəˋmjunjən] *n.* 交流，懇談；宗教；團體

She has a closed communion with nature.

她與大自然親密交融。

communion of interest 共享的利益

6 advance [ədˋvæns] *vi.* 前進；提高　*n.* 進展

That boy advanced on her silently.

那個男孩悄悄地向她走去。

advanced mathematics 高等數學

advance toward sb. 走向某人

pay in advance 預先付款

7 decline [dɪˋklaɪn] *vt.* 下傾；偏斜；衰退

The elector's popularity has declined in the opinion polls.

民調顯示該總統候選人的支持率下滑。

8 tradition [trəˋdɪʃən] *n.* 傳統，慣例

He requested his staff to break the tradition.

他要求他的員工打破傳統。

family tradition 家庭傳統

9 origin [ˋɔrədʒɪn] *n.* 起源；開端

It's a poem about the origin of human beings.

這是一首關於人類起源的詩。

主題 2

10 **future**　[ˋfjutʃɚ]　*n.*　將來，未來

She is indulging in reveries about the future.

她正沉浸於對未來的幻想之中。

future plans 未來的計畫（打算）

future generation 後代們

11 **gaze**　[gez]　*vi.*　凝視，盯，注視

His intent gaze made her uncomfortable.

他的注目凝視使她感到不自在。

gaze upon（目光）凝視在……

gaze at（目光）凝視……

12 **reform**　[ˌrɪˋfɔrm]　*vt.*　*n.*　改革，改良

The citizens made a clamor for reform.

市民強烈要求改革。

reform revolution（社會上的）改革運動

13 **enthusiasm**　[ɪnˋθjuzɪˌæzəm]　*n.*　熱情，熱心，熱忱

Her enthusiasm breathed new life into the club.

她的熱情給社團注入了新的生命。

【同】craze, zeal, passion

【反】apathy

14 **passion**　[ˋpæʃən]　*n.*　激情，熱情；愛好

Nothing could rekindle his extinct passion.

他激情已逝，無從回心轉意。

15 alliance [əˈlaɪəns] *n.* 聯盟，聯合

They forged an alliance.

他們建立同盟。

【同】confederation, association

16 memory [ˈmɛmərɪ] *n.* 記憶；回憶；存儲

My sister has a bad memory for names.

我姊姊對名字的記性很差。

Can a person improve his memory?

一個人能改進他的記憶力嗎？

17 remember [rɪˈmɛmbɚ] *vt.* 記得，想起；記住

I remember seeing her once.

我記得見過她一次。

remember doing sth. 記得做過某事

remember to do sth. 記著去做某事

18 architecture [ˈɑrkəˌtɛktʃɚ] *n.* 建築學；建築式樣

He likes Greek architecture.

他喜歡希臘建築式樣。

19 art [ɑrt] *n.* 藝術；美術

Kelly's mom teaches art history in college.

Kelly 的媽媽在大學教藝術史。

the art of talking 談話術

nature and art 自然與人工

20 **climate**　[ˋklaɪmɪt]　*n.*　氣候；風土，地帶

The girl adapted herself quickly to the new climate.

她很快就適應了這種新氣候。

21 **activity**　[ækˋtɪvətɪ]　*n.*　活動，能動性

The government is concerned about the depression of economic activity.

政府擔憂經濟不景氣。

22 **religion**　[rɪˋlɪdʒən]　*n.*　宗教；宗教信仰

He is unconcerned with questions of religion or morality.

他對宗教問題和道德問題不感興趣。

23 **church**　[tʃɝtʃ]　*n.*　教堂

Is there a church nearby?

附近有教堂嗎？

go to church 去教堂

be in church 在教堂做禮拜

24 **sect**　[sɛkt]　*n.*　（宗教等）派系

Each religious sect in the town has its own church.

該城每一個宗教教派都有自己的教堂。

philosophical sect（哲學界）派系

25 **temple**　[ˋtɛmpl]　*n.*　廟宇；寺院

My foreign friends would like to visit Buddhist temples.

我的外國朋友想去參觀佛寺。

Buddhist Temple 佛寺

26 tabernacle　　[ˋtæbɚ͵næk!]　　*v.*　　臨時住所；禮拜堂

The man was forbidden to walk into the tabernacle.

這男人被禁止走進禮拜堂。

27 worship　　[ˋwɝʃɪp]　　*vt.*　　崇拜　　*vi.*　　做禮拜

The little boy worshipped his father.

這小男孩崇拜他的父親。

主題 2

28 spiritual　　[ˋspɪrɪtʃʊəl]　　*adj.*　　精神的，心靈的

We pursue a life fulfilled with economic and spiritual needs.

我們追求一個滿足經濟和精神雙重需求的生活。

spiritual needs（相對於物質上的）心靈需求

spiritual power 超自然力量

29 historic　　[hɪsˋtɔrɪk]　　*adj.*　　有歷史意義的

This battle is of historic meaning.

這一戰具有歷史意義。

historical site 歷史遺跡

historical fact 史實

30 gallery　　[ˋgælərɪ]　　*n.*　　長廊，遊廊；畫廊

Let's meet at the National Gallery.

我們在國家美術館見。

【同】museum

History 歷史

Track 17

1 beginning [bɪˋgɪnɪŋ] *n.* 開始，開端；起源

You have made a good beginning.

你已經做出了良好的開端。

in the beginning 剛開始的時候

2 historian [hɪsˋtorɪən] *n.* 歷史學家；編史家

The historian searches for primary sources of information about the past.

歷史學家尋找有關過去的原始資料來源。

3 origin [ˋɔrədʒɪn] *n.* 起源；開端

It's a poem about the origin of human beings.

這是一首關於人類起源的詩。

4 heritage [ˋhɛrətɪdʒ] *n.* 遺產，繼承物

It's our duty to protect our national heritage.

保護民族遺產是我們的責任。

5 time [taɪm] *n.* 時間

Only time will tell if you are right.

只有時間才能證明你是否正確。

all the time 一直；始終
on time 準時；不早不晚

6 **pass** [pæs] *v.* 傳遞（用具等）

Pass the salt, please.

請遞給我鹽瓶。

pass on 傳遍，把…傳遞給，傳遞

pass sth. to sb. 把某東西傳給某人

7 **date** [det] *n.* 日期

I have a date tonight.

今晚我有個約會。

dates in history 歷史時期

date back 追溯到

8 **return** [rɪ`tɜˑn] *vi. n.* 回來，返回

She's waiting for the return of winter.

她在等待冬天到來。

return to normal 恢復正常

be returned to 返回到

9 **past** [pæst] *prep.* 過；經過

They walked past without stopping.

他們一步不停地走了過去。

for the past few days 最近幾天

in the past 過去

10 **distant**   [ˋdɪstənt]   *adj.*   在遠處的，疏遠的

This pilgrim came from a very distant place.
這個朝聖者來自非常遠的地方。

be distant from 遠離……

11 **recent**   [ˋrisnt]   *adj.*   新近的，最近的

The house is a recent purchase.
這房子是最近買的。

The growth of industry has been rapid in recent years.
在最近的這些年來工業的成長是非常快速的。

12 **decade**   [ˋdɛked]   *n.*   十年，十年期

We've known each other for decades.
我們已經相識十幾年。

the last decade of the 20th century 20 世紀最後十年（1990-2000）

the red decade 赤色年代（美國 30 年代共產主義氾濫時期）

13 **century**   [ˋsɛntʃʊrɪ]   *n.*   世紀；百年

He mastered the history of the 18th century.
他精通 18 世紀的歷史。

the 21th century 21 世紀

14 **interesting**   [ˋɪntərɪstɪŋ]   *adj.*   有趣的，引人入勝的

What's so interesting?
什麼事這麼有趣？

15 important   [ɪm`pɔrtnt]   *adj.*   重要的；有勢力的

It is important that he needs to face the music.

他必須勇敢面對困難是最重要的。

an important event 一個重大的事件

16 trivial   [`trɪvɪəl]   *adj.*   瑣碎的；平常的

The housewife is tired of doing trivial matters.

家庭主婦厭倦做雜務。

trivial pursuit 一種不斷問問題的問答遊戲

17 possibility   [ˌpɑsə`bɪlətɪ]   *n.*   可能；可能的事

Is there any possibility that we can win this game?

我們有任何贏得這場比賽的勝算嗎？

possibility of raining 降雨率

18 antique   [æn`tik]   *adj.*   古代的   *n.*   古物

Collecting antique plates is her hobby.

收集古盤子是她的興趣。

19 world   [wɝld]   *n.*   世界

He dreams of traveling around the world.

他夢想環遊世界。

around the world 全世界

world-class 世界級的

20 **chronicle** [ˋkrɑnɪk!] *n.* 年代記，記錄，編年史 *vt.* 把……編入編年史

They chronicled the history of this city.

他們記載這座城市的發展史。

21 **event** [ɪˋvɛnt] *n.* 事件，大事；事變

This article discussed the events that led to her suicide.

這篇文章討論了導致她自殺的一系列事件。

22 **tell** [tɛl] *v.* 告訴；講述

Please tell me that joke.

請告訴我那個笑話。

23 **ancient** [ˋenʃənt] *adj.* 古代的，古老的

This is an ancient parable.

這是一個古老的寓言。

ancient history 古代史（指西羅馬帝國滅亡前的歐洲歷史）

24 **tale** [tel] *n.* 傳說；故事

Kids always like to listen to the fairy tales.

小孩都喜歡聽童話故事。

25 **sage** [sedʒ] *adj.* 智慧的 *n.* 智者

Confucius is considered the greatest of the ancient Chinese sages.

孔子被認為是中國古代最偉大的聖賢。

26 ago　　[əˋgo]　　*adv.*　以前

She and her husband met 2 years ago.

她和她先生在兩年前認識的。

a long time ago 很久以前

27 legend　　[ˋlɛdʒənd]　　*n.*　傳說，傳奇

He is the hero of an old legend.

他是一個古老傳說中的英雄。

28 fact　　[fækt]　　*n.*　事實；實際

Nothing can threaten the fact.

事實不受威脅。

be astonished at the fact that 對……的那個事實感到震驚

29 learn　　[lɝn]　　*vi.*　*vt.*　學，學習

He has learnt a new skill.

他學會了一項新技能。

learn about sth. 瞭解（學習）某事

learn sth. by heart 背誦某東西

learn a lesson 得到教訓

30 example　　[ɪgˋzæmpl]　　*n.*　例子；榜樣

Their courage was an example to all of us.

他們的勇氣是我們大家學習的榜樣。

give sb. an example 給某人舉個例子

follow one's example 以某人為榜樣

主題 **2**

Economy 經濟

Track 18

1　stable　[`steb!]　*adj.*　穩定的，不變的

A stable government is essential to economic growth.

穩定的政府對經濟增長是重要的。

2　economy　[ɪ`kɑnəmɪ]　*n.*　經濟；節約，節省

The nation's economy is growing rapidly.

這個國家的經濟在快速增長。

3　recovery　[rɪ`kʌvɚ]　*n.*　重新獲得；挽回

Annie made a quick recovery from her illness.

安妮很快地病癒。

4　depression　[dɪ`prɛʃən]　*n.*　沮喪；不景氣，蕭條

She suffered from depression.

她深受憂鬱症的折磨。

The Great Depression 1920-1930 的全球經濟大恐慌

5　dismiss　[dɪs`mɪs]　*vt.*　打發走；開除

He was dismissed from his job.

他被開除了。

6 employ [ɪm`plɔɪ] *vi.* 雇用；使用

He has fifteen workers in his employ.

他雇用的工人有十五名。

be employed to do sth. 被雇用去做某事

7 rate [ret] *n.* 比率；速率；等級

The unemployment rate is rising in that country.

那個國家的失業率正在上升。

8 flounder [`flaʊndɚ] *v.* 掙扎，艱苦地移動

Many corporations are floundering.

許多企業舉步維艱。

9 index [`ɪndɛks] *n.* 索引；指數；指標

The book is not well indexed.

這部書索引做得不好。

index card（圖書館的）索引目錄卡

index finger 食指

10 govern [`gʌvənmənt] *vt.* 統治；控制

Who governs that company?

誰治理那間公司？

You should govern your temper.

你應該要控制好自己的脾氣。

11 **regulate**　[ˋrɛgjəˌlet]　*n.*　管理；使規則化

The supervisor regulates the employees of his department.

上司規範他部門的員工。

Regulating your eating habits is good for your health.

使飲食習慣規律化有益於健康。

12 **spur**　[spɝ]　*n.*　刺激物　*vt.*　刺激

The election was a spur to the ruling party to respond to public opinion.

這次選舉刺激執政黨回應公眾輿論。

【同】goad, activate, provoke

【反】curb, discourage

13 **grow**　[gro]　*vi.*　生長；變得；增長

His cold is growing worse.

他的感冒正在加重。

grow up 成年，長大成人

14 **slowly**　[sloli]　*adj.*　慢的；遲鈍的

The manager didn't have any choice, so he nodded slowly and said "yes".

經理沒有任何選擇，他只好慢慢地點頭說：「好」。

15 **thrifty**　[ˋθrɪftɪ]　*adj.*　節儉的；興旺的

My mother is thrifty.

我媽媽很節儉。

thrift shop 二手商店、低價商店

16 **impediment**　[ɪm`pɛdəmənt]　*n.*　妨礙，阻礙物

War has been an impediment to progress.

戰爭成了進步的阻礙。

speech impediment 口吃

17 **commerce**　[`kɑmɝs]　*n.*　商業，貿易；社交

The student wants to major in international commerce in college.

這個學生大學想主修國際貿易。

overseas commerce 海外貿易

18 **exchange**　[ɪks`tʃendʒ]　*vt.*　交換；交流　*n.*　交換

You will have a chance to exchange your viewpoints at tomorrow's meeting.

明天你們將會在會議上交換看法。

19 **profit**　[`prɑfɪt]　*n.*　益處；利潤　*vi.*　得益

There is very little profit in selling newspapers at present.

現在賣報紙利潤很少。

net profit 淨利；純利

profit margin 利潤比率

20 **loss**　[lɔs]　*n.*　遺失；損失；失敗

It is a great loss to her.

這是她的巨大損失。

The loss of his money worried him.

他的錢遺失使他擔心。

21 payment　[ˋpemənt]　*n.*　支付，支付的款項

The payment of the goods is payable in installments.
貨款可以分期支付。

22 finance　[faɪˋnæns]　*vt.*　提供資金

He is a well-known expert in finance.
他是知名的金融專家。

23 resource　[rɪˋsors]　*n.*　資源

Hank is a person of great resource. When I don't know
what to do, I will ask him for his advice.
Hank 是一個足智多謀的人，當我不知道該怎麼做的時候，我會問他的
意見。

24 credit　[ˋkrɛdɪt]　*n.*　信用貸款；信用

Sam doesn't have enough money to buy the furniture, so
he decides to buy it on credit.
Sam 沒有足夠的錢買傢俱，所以他決定辦信貸購買。
Don't give credit to what the woman said.
不要相信那女人說的。

25 project　[prəˋdʒɛkt]　*n.*　企劃；專案

Our supervisor divided us into two groups, and he wanted
each group to work on a project.
我們的主管把我們分成 2 組，他想要每一組作一個專案。

26 **manufacture** [ˌmænjəˈfæktʃɚ] *vt.* 製造 *n.* 製造；產品

The manufacture of these small components is expensive.
製造這些小零件是非常昂貴的。

27 **produce** [prəˈdjus] *vt.* 生產；產生；展現

The factory produces 1,000 cars a week.
這家工廠每星期生產一千輛轎車。
produce maps 繪製地圖
produce goods 生產商品

主題 2

28 **free** [fri] *adj.* 自由的；空閒的

Is he free to leave now?
他現在可以離開了嗎？
be free 有空的，空閒的，免費
be set free 被釋放

29 **control** [kənˈtrol] *vt. n.* 控制；支配

Inflation has gotten out of control.
通貨膨脹失去了控制。
control one's anger 控制某人的憤怒
go out of control 失控

30 **goal** [gol] *n.* 目標，終點，球門，得分

They reached the goal on the last day of their trip.
他們在旅程的最後一天到達了終點。
【同】destination, intent, target

International 國際

 Track 19

1　whole [hol] *adj.* 整個的

The whole village was anxious for rescue.

全村上下都渴望救援。

whole-heartedly 全心全意地，專心地，摯誠地

2　absolute [ˋæbsə,lut] *adj.* 絕對的；純粹的

There's no absolute answer for the question.

這個問題沒有絕對的答案。

She has absolute faith in my judgment.

她完全信賴我的判斷。

absolute majority 絕對多數

3　permanent [ˋpɝmənənt] *adj.* 永久的，持久的

The family is looking for a permanent place to live.

這家人正在找固定的居所。

permanent address 固定地址

4　goodwill [ˋɡʊdˋwɪl] *n.* 善意，親切；親善

The charity relies on the goodwill of the donators to help it raise money.

這個慈善機構仰賴捐款者來幫忙集資。

a goodwill gesture 示好

5 **oblige**   [ə`blaɪdʒ]   *vt.*   強迫；迫使

The scandal obliged the singer to retire.

這一醜聞迫使這名歌手引退。

6 **along**   [ə`lɔŋ]   *prep.*   沿著   *adv.*   向前

We walked along the road.

我們沿著路走。

come along with sb. 和某人一起來

get along with 過生活、相處

7 **exploration**   [ˌɛksplə`reʃən]   *n.*   考察；勘探；探查

Scientists began the exploration of new planets.

科學家開始了對新星球的探索。

The exploration for new sources of energy is important for the future of the Earth.

新能源的研究對地球的未來很重要。

8 **onward**   [`ɑnwəd]   *adv.*   向前地，前進地

The business is moving onward.

商業正向前發展。

upward 向上地

9 **usual**   [`juʒʊəl]   *adj.*   通常的；平常的

He went to school later than usual.

他比平時晚到校。

主題 2

as usual 像平常一樣

10 **stately** ［ˋstetlɪ］ *adj.* 莊嚴的；雄偉的；堂皇的

The hall in the castle was grand and stately.

城堡裡的大廳輝煌而莊嚴。

a stately procession 威嚴的隊伍

11 **statesman** ［ˋstetsmən］ *n.* 政治家，國務活動家

He is known as a statesman.

他是知名的政治家。

elder statesman（政界）元老

12 **nation** ［ˋneʃən］ *n.* 民族；國家

Germany is one of the leading industrialized nations.

德國是工業化國家之一。

13 **decay** ［dɪˋke］ *vt.* *vi.* （使）腐朽，（使）腐爛

Pollution has decayed the sea wall.

汙染已經侵蝕了防波堤。

fall into decay 結構或身體惡化

14 **crumble** ［ˋkrʌmb!］ *vt.* *vi.* 弄碎，崩毀

The child crumbled some cookies in her fingers.

小孩用手指捏碎了一些餅乾。

The big earthquake crumbled many houses.

強烈地震震垮了許多房子。

15 **strife** [straɪf] *n.* 衝突，競爭

What is the major cause of the civil strife?

市民的衝突的主要原因是什麼？

family strife 家庭不和

16 **brink** [brɪŋk] *n.* （峭壁的）邊沿，邊緣

The president brought the country to the brink of war.

總統把國家帶到了戰爭邊緣。

17 **plight** [plaɪt] *n.* 困境

The television show brought us all the plight of the refugees.

我們從電視節目知道了難民所處的一切困境。

plight of the poor 窮人的困境

18 **revolt** [rɪˋvolt] *vi.* *n.* 反抗，造反

The supports revolted when the senator lost the election.

當那名議員輸了選舉，支持者們開始造反。

revolt against… 反抗……

19 **abolish** [əˋbɑlɪʃ] *vt.* 廢除，取消

There are many bad rules of the school that ought to be abolished.

學校有許多不良的規定應予以廢除。

20 **declare** [dɪˋklɛr] *vt.* 斷言；聲明；表明

The manager declared for their proposal.

經理宣布贊成他們的建議。

declare the meeting open 宣佈會議開始

declare that... 宣佈……

21 **independence** [ˌɪndɪˋpɛndəns] *n.* 獨立，自主，自立

The young man tried to preserve his independence.

年輕人試圖保持自己的獨立性。

22 **toil** [tɔɪl] *n.* *vi.* 辛苦，辛勤勞作

The man succeeded after years of toil.

那人經歷數年的辛勞之後成功了。

hard toil 努力

a life of toil 勞苦的一生

23 **crush** [krʌʃ] *vt.* 壓碎，碾碎；鎮壓

The rebellion was crushed by military forces.

軍隊已把叛亂鎮壓下去。

My mom crushed garlic with a knife.

媽媽用刀壓碎大蒜。

crush on 著迷

24 **spy** [spaɪ] *n.* 間諜，特務 *vt.* 偵察

This evidence shows that he is a spy.

這個證據證實了他是間諜。

spy on sth. / sb. 監視……

25 **cunning** [ˋkʌnɪŋ] *adj.* 狡猾的，狡詐的

Do not believe in him. He is cunning.

別相信他，他很狡猾。

26 journal [`dʒɝn!] *n.* 日報，雜誌；日誌

The journal publishes once every two months.

這本刊物兩個月出版一次。

keep a journal 寫日記

27 news [njuz] *n.* 新聞，消息

Have you read the news about the game?

你看了關於球賽的新聞了嗎？

28 expose [ɪk`spoz] *vt.* 使暴露；揭露

The reporter was killed because he exposed a plot of the politician.

這名記者因為揭露一個政客的陰謀而被殺害。

expose to 遭受，曝露於

expose oneself 走光

29 startle [`stɑrt!] *vt.* *vi.* 使大吃一驚 *n.* 吃驚

He was startled by the bad news.

這壞消息使他大吃一驚。

be startled to do sth. 因某事而感到震驚

30 deed [did] *n.* 行為；事蹟

Her deed is contemptible.

她的行為是可輕視的。

Business 商業

1　organize　[`ɔrgə,naɪz]　*vi.　vt.*　組織，編組

The meeting was organized by students.
這個會議是由學生組織的。

organize yourself 自我組織

2　extensive　[ɪk`stɛnsɪv]　*adj.*　廣闊的；廣泛的

They own extensive land by the forest.
他們擁有森林邊的遼闊土地。

Flooding has caused extensive damage to the town.
洪水對城鎮造成廣泛的破壞。

extensive coverage 大篇幅

3　headquarters　[`hɛd`kwɔrtɚz]　*n.*　司令部；總部

The company's headquarters is in New York.
這家公司的總部在紐約。

general headquarters 總部

4　prosperous　[`prɑspərəs]　*adj.*　繁榮的，昌盛的

The small business soon became very prosperous.
小企業很快就變得非常興旺。

5 prospect   [`prɑspɛkt]   *n.*   展望；前景，前程

This journey opened a new prospect in his mind.

這一旅程為他的思想開闊了新的視野。

prospect of doing sth. 對做……充滿展望

job prospects 職涯前景

6 talent   [`tælənt]   *n.*   天才；才能；人才

She's got such talent for singing.

她對歌唱有非凡的才能。

7 yearly   [`jɪrlɪ]   *adj.*   每年的   *adv.*   一年一度

The yearly conference will start in five minutes.

年會將於五分鐘後開始。

The rent was paid yearly.

房租每年付一次。

8 integrity   [ɪn`tɛgrətɪ]   *n.*   誠實，正直

She is keen to preserve her professional integrity.

她十分重視保持自己的職業操守。

moral integrity 道德

political integrity 政治正義

9 devotion   [dɪ`voʃən]   *n.*   獻身；忠誠；專心

The teacher always shows her devotion to children.

老師總是展現對小孩的奉獻精神。

10 **watchful** [`wɑtʃfəl] *adj.* 注意的，警惕的

We should be watchful of strangers.

我們應該警惕陌生人。

keep a watchful eye on 關心，注意

under one's watchful eyes 遵循某人的指示

11 **temporary** [`tɛmpə,rɛrɪ] *adj.* 暫時的；臨時的

His blindness was only temporary.

他的失明只是暫時的。

12 **rival** [`raɪv!] *n.* 競爭者 *adj.* 競爭的

Tim has some rivals for this job.

有幾個競爭者與提姆在爭這份工作。

rival company 競爭公司

arch-rival 主要對手

13 **diminish** [də`mɪnɪʃ] *vt.* 減少，減小，遞減

Our food supply has diminished as a result of the famine.

由於飢荒我們的食物供給減少了

diminishing returns 報酬遞減

diminished responsibility 減輕刑事責任

14 **beget** [bɪ`gɛt] *vt.* 產生，引起

Earthquake begets misery and ruin.

地震帶來苦難與毀滅。

15 **discussion** [dɪ`skʌʃən] *n.* 討論，談論；論述

The point of the disscussion group is about western history.

小組討論的重點是有關於西方歷史。

under discussion 討論中

16 gloomy   [ˋglumɪ] *adj.*   黑暗的；令人沮喪的

Gleams of sunshine lit up the gloomy morning.

陽光使陰暗的早晨明亮起來。

17 disposition   [ˌdɪspəˋzɪʃən] *n.*   處理，天性、氣質

Linda had a gentle, modest disposition.

琳達性格溫柔而謙虛。

of a nervous disposition 有神經質

have a cheerful disposition 有爽朗的性格

18 slander   [ˋslændɚ] *n.*   *vt.*   誹謗，詆毀

The manager claims she was slandered at the meeting.

經理聲稱她在會議上受人詆毀。

be sued for slander 因毀謗而被起訴

19 proclaim   [prəˋklem] *vt.*   宣告，宣佈；表明

The minister proclaimed the new policy.

部長宣布新政策。

proclaim sb. sth. 宣告某人成為……

20 bid   [bɪd] *vt.*   命令 *vi.*   報價

Do as your parents bid.

照父母的吩咐去做。

Michelle knew she can't afford the car, so she didn't bid.

米雪兒知道她負擔不起這部車，所以她沒出價。

21 **bribe** [braɪb] *n.* 賄賂 *vt.* 向……行賄

It's impossible for me to accept a bribe.

我絕不收賄。

Hank bribed the local officials to run an illegal company.

漢克賄賂地方官員以便經營一家違法公司。

22 **chamber** [`tʃembɚ] *n.* 會議室；房間；腔

The council chamber has a gallery for guests.

這個會議室設有聽眾席。

chamber of commerce 商會

23 **justify** [`dʒʌstə,faɪ] *vt.* 證明 … 是正當的

The thief can't justify his action.

小偷無法證明他的行為是正當。

justify yourself 為自己辯護

24 **monopoly** [mə`nɑplɪ] *n.* 壟斷，獨佔，專利

No one could compete with these media monopolies.

沒有人能和這些媒體壟斷企業競爭。

25 **former** [`fɔrmɚ] *adj.* 在前的 *n.* 前者

In former days, there was a gym here.

從前這兒有個體育館。

Of these two skirts, I prefer the former.

這二件裙子，我喜歡前者。

26 **treasurer** [ˋtrɛʒərə] *n.* 司庫，財務主管

Who can we have as treasurer?
我們能讓誰掌管財務呢？

27 **boldness** [ˋboldnɪs] *n.* 大膽，勇敢，冒失

The captain was honored by his boldness in sailing into an enemy harbor to attack their ships.
船長因駕船駛進敵人港口攻擊敵艦的勇敢所被推崇。

28 **redress** [rɪˋdrɛs] *n.* *vt.* 改正，修正

The student did all that he could do to redress these mistakes.
學生盡可能地補償這些錯誤。

redress the situation 改變情況

29 **stay** [ste] *vi.* 停留；暫住

Peter stayed late at the office last night.
昨晚彼得在辦公室待到很晚。

30 **readily** [ˋrɛdɪlɪ] *adv.* 樂意地；無困難地

These problems are not readily solvable.
這些問題不容易解決。

The lady readily accepts my invitation.
女士欣然地接受我的邀約。

Media 媒體

Track 21

1 **medium** [ˋmidɪəm] *n.* 媒質；中間 *adj.* 中等的

The man is of medium height.

這男人中等個兒。

medium of exchange 交易媒介

2 **anticipate** [ænˋtɪsəˌpet] *vt.* 預料，預期，期望

It is possible for to us anticipate when it will happen.

我們可以預料這事何時發生。

anticipate changes / developments 預料改變或發展

3 **unfold** [ʌnˋfold] *vt.* 展開 *vi.* 呈現

The plot unfolds as the movie goes on.

隨著電影的放映，故事情節展開了。

The traveler unfolded the map.

旅行者展開地圖。

4 **send** [sɛnd] *vt.* *vi.* 送

Mark sent the letter by sea.

馬克將信以海運寄送。

send sth. to sb. 將某物寄給某人

send sth. by post 郵寄某物

5 forth [forθ] *adv.* 向前；向外，往外

He set forth on his journey this July.
他今年七月啟程旅行。

6 skillful [`skɪlfəl] *adj.* 靈巧的，嫻熟的

He is skillful in the use of the hands.
他善於手的使用。

Robert is a skillful baseball player.
羅伯是一位有技巧的棒球員。

skillful at (doing) sth. 對……很熟練

主題 2

7 zealous [`zɛləs] *adj.* 熱心的，熱情的

She is a zealous card player.
她是位玩撲克牌狂熱者。

Lucas is a zealous supporter of religious activities.
盧卡斯對宗教活動很熱心。

be zealous in (doing) sth. 對於……很熱心

8 announcer [ə`naʊnsɚ] *n.* 宣告者；播音員

The announcer led with the day's headlines.
播音員以一天中的頭條新聞開始。

9 recount [ˌri`kaʊnt] *vt.* 描述，敘述

Lauren recounted her experience.
羅倫講了她的經歷。

Ken recounted how he and Lisa met.
肯敘述他和麗莎怎麼認識。

10 **urgent** ［`ɝdʒənt］ *adj.* 緊急的；　求的

These patients are in urgent need of medical attention.
這患者急需醫學救援。
urgent action 緊急行動

11 **article** ［`ɑrtɪk!］ *n.* 文章，論文；冠詞

Jackson has written an article for the journal.
傑克森已為期刊撰寫了一篇文章。

12 **slant** ［slænt］ *vi.* 傾斜

The plumber slanted the pipe to allow water to run off.
水管工使管子傾斜以便泄水。
The sunshine slanted through the window.
陽光從窗戶照進來。

13 **accomplish** ［ə`kɑmplɪʃ］ *vt.* 達到（目的）；完成

Allen didn't accomplish the task.
艾倫沒有完成任務。
The students have accomplished what they set out to do.
學生們完成他們所設定的目標。
mission accomplished 目標達成

14 **scoop** ［skup］ *n.* 鏟子，勺子，獨家新聞，穴

My mom bought several scoops in the supermarket.
媽媽在超市買了好幾個勺子。
What's the scoop?
有什麼新鮮事？

15 **calamity** [kə`læmətɪ] *n.* 大災禍，不幸之事

A series of calamities destroyed the city.

一連串的災禍催毀了這城市。

16 **swarm** [swɔrm] *n.* 一大群 *vi.* 密集

The singer left amid a swarm of reporters.

歌手離開時一群記者圍著她。

A swarm of bees attacked the hiker.

一群蜜蜂攻擊健行者。

17 **suspect** [sə`spɛkt] *vt.* *vi.* 懷疑 *n.* 嫌疑犯

Hank is a prime suspect in the robbery case.

漢克是這宗劫案的主嫌犯。

18 **confusion** [kən`fjuʒən] *n.* 混亂；騷亂；混淆

The stadium was in confusion after the concert.

演唱會之後，體育館裡一片混亂。

create / lead to confusion 製造混亂

19 **agitation** [ˌædʒə`teʃən] *n.* 鼓動，煽動；攪動

The agitation for a strike arose repeatedly.

罷工風潮迭起。

Jenny was in a state of agitation.

珍妮十分激動。

agitation against 鼓噪反對

20 **righteousness** [ˋraɪtʃəsnɪs] *n.* 正義，公正，正直

Some people spend time looking after righteousness, but they cannot find any time to practice it.

有些人花費時間搜尋正義，卻騰不出時間來付諸實踐。

21 **remind** [rɪˋmaɪnd] *vt.* 使想起

The lovely girl reminds me of my sister.

這位可愛的女孩使我想起了我妹妹。

remind sb. about sth. 使某人想起某事

22 **nightly** [ˋnaɪtlɪ] *adj. adv.* 每夜的，夜間的

The game was broadcast nightly.

這場賽是每晚轉播。

23 **scant** [skænt] *adj.* 不足的，缺乏的

The swimmer paid scant attention to the lifeguard's warnings.

游泳者沒注意到救生員的警告。

24 **augment** [ɔgˋmɛnt] *vi. vt.* 增大，增值

She tries to find a part-time job to augment her income.

她嘗試找兼差增加自己的收入。

25 **majority** [məˋdʒɔrətɪ] *n.* 多數；大多數

The majority of children seem to prefer chocolate to coffee.

多數孩童喜歡巧克力勝過咖啡。

26 mighty [`maɪtɪ] *adj.* 強大的；巨大的

Once upon a time, a mighty empire ruled the world.

一個強大的帝國曾統治世界。

27 lull [lʌl] *vt.* 使安靜

My father used to lull me to sleep when I was little.

小時候，爸爸總哄我入睡。

lull sb. into (doing) sth. 讓某人感到……

28 fickle [`fɪk!] *adj.* （愛情或友誼上）易變的，不堅定的

Luke is a fickle lover.

路克是個用情不專的愛人。

29 administration [əd,mɪnə`streʃən] *n.* 局（或署、處等），管理，行政

I hate the inefficient administration.

我痛恨無效率的行政機關。

30 masquerade [,mæskə`red] *n.* 化裝舞會 *vi.* 偽裝

They are going to join in the masquerade this weekend.

他們週末要去參加化裝舞會。

Community 社區

Track 22

1 boon [bun] *n.* 恩惠

The extra rain was a boon to the crops.

這場臨時雨是農作物的福音。

boon companion 好友

2 abode [ə`bod] *n.* 住處，住所

I invite some friends to my sweet abode.

我邀請一些朋友來我甜蜜的家。

right of abode 居留權

3 among [ə`mʌŋ] *prep.* 在……之中

Bob has always been popular among his colleagues.

鮑伯在同事中一直很受歡迎。

I saw one of my friends among the crowd.

我在群眾中看見一位朋友。

among yourselves / themselves / ourselves 互相

4 desirable [dɪ`zaɪrəb!] *adj.* 值得相望的；可取的

The ability to have some familiarity with computers is desirable.

熟悉電腦技能是需要的。

a highly desirable job 極令人嚮往的工作

5 life [laɪf] *n.* 生命，生活

There is no life on the sun.

太陽上沒有生物。

give one's life for 為⋯⋯而獻出生命（獻身）

6 liberty [ˋlɪbɚtɪ] *n.* 自由；釋放；許可

For my love I will sacrifice life, for liberty I will sacrifice my love.

【詩】生命誠可貴，愛情價更高；若為自由故，兩者皆可拋。

Thousands of prisoners are to be given their liberty.

數千個囚犯被釋放。

take the liberty of doing sth. 未經允許做⋯⋯

civil liberty 公民自由

7 little [ˋlɪt!] *adj.* 少的，小的

Steven is too little to drink alcohol.

史蒂芬太小了，不能喝酒。

This little room is too crowded for me.

這間小房間對我來說太擠了。

a little bit 一點；稍微

8 haven [ˋhevən] *n.* 安息所，避難所

The kind man has made his home a haven for homeless orphans.

善心人把自己的家變成了無家可歸的孤兒們的避難所。

9　**alive** 　[əˋlaɪv]　*adj.*　活著

The injured man fainted but is still alive.
受傷的人昏了過去但仍活著。
bring sth. alive 使……有趣

10　**thrive** 　[θraɪv]　*vi.*　興旺，繁榮，旺盛

He that will thrive must rise at five.
【諺】五更起床，百事興旺。

11　**adjoin** 　[əˋdʒɔɪn]　*vt.*　貼近，毗連；靠近

A plot of land adjoins our house.
一塊地與我們的房子毗連。

12　**then** 　[ðɛn]　*adv.*　那時

The couple lived in the small village then.
那對夫妻當時住在一個小村莊。

13　**robber** 　[ˋrɑbɚ]　*n.*　強盜，盜賊

The robber shot one police officer and ran away.
強盜射中一名警察就逃走了。

14　**criminal** 　[ˋkrɪmənḷ]　*n.*　犯人，罪犯，刑事犯　*adj.*　犯罪的

That criminal was finally sentenced to death.
那個罪犯終於被判處死刑。

15　**prey** 　[pre]　*vi.*　捕獲　*n.*　獵物

The frog fell a prey to the snake.

青蛙成了蛇的獵物。

Cats prey on mice.

貓捕食老鼠。

prey on one's mind 使擔憂

16 captive [`kæptɪv] *n.* 俘虜，被監禁的人 *adj.* 被俘虜的

The kid was held captive for a week.

這小孩被監禁了一星期。

Rick is a captive to Lisa's charms.

瑞克被麗莎的魅力所俘虜。

hold / take sb. captive 監禁某人

17 agitate [`ædʒə,tet] *vi.* 煽動；鼓動

The president's fiery speech agitated the crowd.

總統激昂的演說鼓動了聽眾。

agitate for / against 煽動

18 discourse [`dɪskors] *n.* 講話，演說，講道

The audience listened to his discourse on global warming.

聽眾聽他作關於全球暖化的演講。

a discourse on / upon 關於……的演講

19 villain [`vɪlən] *n.* 壞人，惡棍

The killer is a murderous villain.

那個殺人犯是個窮凶極惡的暴徒。

the villain of the piece 罪魁禍首

20 trial　[`traɪəl]　*n.*　試，試驗；審判

The criminal's on trial for his life.

罪犯正在受決定他生死的審判。

21 witness　[`wɪtnɪs]　*n.*　證據；證人　*vt.*　目擊

She was the witness to the argument.

她是這場爭論的證人。

Some citizens claimed to witness the attack.

一些市民宣稱目擊這攻擊。

key witness 主要證人

22 attorney　[ə`tɝnɪ]　*n.*　代理人；辯護律師

My brother is an attorney. He has his own practice.

我哥哥是律師。他自己開業。

23 assert　[ə`sɝt]　*vt.*　斷言，宣稱；維護

Nowadays women assert themselves politically.

現今的女性護衛自己的政治權。

assert your right 維護自我權利

24 plead　[plid]　*vt.*　為……辯護　*vi.*　抗辯

He forgot his homework again, and pled ignorance.

他以忘記為藉口又忘了帶作業。

plead guilty / innocent 辯稱有罪或無罪

25 discharge　[dɪs`tʃɑrdʒ]　*vt.*　釋放；排出　*n.*　釋放

The judge discharged the prisoner.

法官把囚犯釋放了。

discharge sb. from sth. 把……從某處釋放

discharge into river 排入河裡

26 iniquity [ɪ`nɪkwətɪ] *n.* 邪惡，不公正

The club is a den of iniquity.

這個俱樂部是一個充滿罪惡的場所。

human justice and iniquity 人類的正義與邪惡

主題 2

27 protest [prə`tɛst] *vt.* *vi.* *n.* 抗議

Victor's protests on human rights sound solid.

維克就人權問題提出的抗議聽來很有力。

under protest 不願意地；在抗議下

28 desolation [ˌdɛs!`eʃən] *n.* 荒蕪，荒廢，荒涼

Jack was startled when he saw the desolation caused by the tsunami.

看到海嘯造成的荒涼，傑克感到觸目驚心。

29 empty [`ɛmptɪ] *adj.* 空的；空洞的

My brother moved to Paris and his room is empty.

我哥哥搬去巴黎，現在他的房間是空的。

30 destruction [dɪ`strʌkʃən] *n.* 破壞，毀滅，消滅

Not to protest is to sit idle watching the destruction of the environment.

對於破壞環境的行為不加反對就等於縱容。

Unit
11

Advertising 廣告

Track 23

1 **solemn**　[ˋsɑləm]　*adj.*　莊嚴的；隆重的

The ceremony was a solemn event.

這場典禮是一件隆重的大事。

solemn ritual 莊重的儀式

2 **cordial**　[ˋkɔrdʒəl]　*adj.*　真誠的，誠懇的

The owner of the villa gave us a cordial greeting.

度假別墅的主人熱忱地歡迎我們。

The meeting was conducted in a cordial atmosphere.

會議以熱忱的氣氛進行。

a cordial smile 一個真摯的微笑

3 **charm**　[tʃɑrm]　*n.*　魅力；嫵媚　*vi.*　迷人

The woman's gentle personality is her greatest charm.

那女人溫柔的個性是她最迷人之處。

They were charmed by the kindness of the villagers.

他們被村民的仁慈所吸引。

charm school 美姿美儀學校

4 **boast**　[bost]　*vi.*　自誇　*vt.*　吹噓

The woman boasted that her daughter was a genius.

那女人吹噓自己的女兒是天才。

boast about 自誇有關……

5 **survey** [sə`ve] *vt.* 俯瞰；檢查；測量

The driver got out of the car to survey the damage.

駕駛從車裡出來檢查損壞。

6 **embroider** [ɪm`brɔɪdə] *vi.* *vt.* 刺繡，修飾

My grandma embroiders very well.

我祖母很會刺繡。

The skirt was embroidered with flowers.

這件裙上繡了花朵。

embroider sth. on sth. 將……刺繡在……上

7 **characteristic** [ˌkærəktə`rɪstɪk] *adj.* 特有的 *n.* 特性

I can't live with the characteristic noises of cities.

我無法忍受都市特有的喧囂。

Diligent images are a distinguishing characteristic of Debby's work.

勤勉的形象是黛比與別人不同的特色。

defining characteristic 區別的特色

8 **expectation** [ˌɛkspɛk`teʃən] *n.* 期待，期望，預期

She ate a light lunch in expectation of losing some weight.

她午飯吃得很少，期待可以瘦一些。

above / below expectations 高或低於期望

主題 2

come / live up to one's expectations 達到……的期待

9 **difference**　[`dɪfərəns]　*n.*　差別；差；分歧

Decoration makes no difference to this house.

這房子有沒有花裝潢沒什麼區別。

have a difference of opinion ……意見有分歧

the difference between 在……不同（差別）

10 **though**　[ðo]　*adv. conj.*　雖然

Though he is almost 50, his face still looks young.

他雖然快五十歲，但他的臉看起來仍然年輕。

The house, though old, is pleasant.

這房子雖小卻很舒適。

11 **absurd**　[əb`sɝd]　*adj.*　不合理的，荒唐的

Elsa's opinion is absurd.

愛爾莎的意見是愚蠢可笑的。

12 **retail**　[`ritel]　*n.*　零售　*adj.*　零售的

Please tell me the retail price of these skirts.

請告訴我這些裙子的零售價。

retail trade / business 零售業

retail elephant 零售巨頭

13 **almost**　[`ɔl,most]　*adv.*　幾乎

Dinner is almost ready.

晚餐差不多準備好了。

14 **either**   [ˋiðɚ]   *conj.*   或者

Can you speak either Italian or Spanish?

你會說義大利語或西班牙語嗎？

15 **appeal**   [əˋpil]   *vi.*   *n.*   呼籲；申述

My boss appealed his case to the local court.

我老闆向上地方法院申訴他的案件。

The police issued an appeal to the crowd to stay away from the building on fire.

警察呼籲群眾遠離著火的建築物。

appeal to 向……呼籲；訴諸於

16 **vanity**   [ˋvænətɪ]   *n.*   虛榮心，虛誇

He bought the necklace to flatter his girlfriends' vanity.

他買項鍊以滿足他女朋友的虛榮心。

vanity case 小化妝箱

17 **avarice**   [ˋævərɪs]   *n.*   貪財，貪婪

Avarice drove Nick into theft.

貪婪驅使尼克偷竊。

18 **impress**   [ɪmˋprɛs]   *vt.*   印；留下極深的印象

Anita impressed me as an artist.

她給我留下了藝術家的印象。

impress sth. on sb. 某事使某人印象深刻

19 reader　[ˋridɚ]　*n.*　讀者；讀物，讀本

I am a regular reader of this magazine.

我是這雜誌的長期讀者。

20 afraid　[əˋfred]　*adj.*　（口語）怕，害怕

I can't help you, I'm afraid.

我恐怕幫不了你的忙，對不起。

21 great　[gret]　*adj.*　偉大的；重大的

It's a great idea!

好主意！

22 mean　[min]　*vt.*　意思是……；意指

Justin meant no harm.

賈斯丁沒有惡意。

23 fruitful　[ˋfrutfəl]　*adj.*　收益好的；肥沃的

The auction was fruitful and resulted in a lot of income.

這拍賣會的銷售卓有成效並產生大量的收入。

a busy and fruitful time 忙碌且充實的時間

24 scourge　[skɚdʒ]　*n.*　*vt.*　鞭笞，磨難

The prisoner is scourged by a guilty conscience.

這個囚犯受到負罪感的折磨。

scourge for 嚴斥

25 extension   [ɪkˋstɛnʃən]   *n.*   延長部分；伸展

George is been given an extension to finish his thesis.
喬治得到完成論文的延長期限。

by extension 延伸來說

26 consequent   [ˋkɑnsəˏkwɛnt]   *adj.*   作為結果的；必然的

The rise in inflation will cause consequent fall in demand.
物價上漲會造成需求必然減少。

27 evident   [ˋɛvədənt]   *adj.*   明顯的，明白的

It's evident to me that Allen isn't telling the truth.
我看得出來艾倫未說出實情。

self-evident 不證自明

28 use   [juz]   *vt.*   用；耗費   *n.*   用

He makes good use of his time.
他能充分利用時間。

29 unwelcome   [ʌnˋwɛlkəm]   *adj.*   不受歡迎的，不被喜歡的

We told Cathy directly that she was unwelcome.
我們直接地告訴凱西大家不歡迎她。

30 everlasting   [ˏɛvəˋlæstɪŋ]   *adj.*   永久的；持久的

Ancient emperors had a belief in life everlasting.
古代皇帝有永生的信念。

everlasting fame 永生名譽

Opinion 意見評論

Track 24

1 different [`dɪfərənt] *adj.* 不同的

Western culture is different from ours.

西方文化與我們的不同。

be different from 與⋯⋯不同

2 utterance [`ʌtərəns] *n.* 說話，發表，說話的方式，死

Artists are judged by their public utterances.

人們會藉由藝人在公開場合的發言來判斷他們。

Gina's utterance reveals her emotion.

吉娜的發言顯露出她的情緒。

give utterance to one's views 發表自己的觀點

3 remark [rɪ`mɑrk] *vt.* *vi.* *n.* 評論，談論

The professor remarked that the essay was well-written.

教授評論說那篇申論寫得很好。

The minister refused to make the remark.

部長拒絕做評論。

critical remark 批判的評論

4 alike [ə`laɪk] *adj.* 同樣的，相同的　*adv.* 相同地

The twins look much alike.

這對雙胞胎看上去非常相像。

great mind think alike 智者所見略同

5　believe　[bɪˋliv]　*vt.*　相信；認為

My boss believed in my ability.

我老闆相信我的才幹。

believe sb. to be ... 相信某人是……

It is believed that 根據……，有人相信……，人們相信……

6　whose　[huz]　*pron.*　誰的；哪個人的

Whose bag is this?

這是誰的袋子？

7　explanation　[͵ɛkspləˋneʃən]　*n.*　解釋，說明；辯解

I think that your explanation is logical.

我想你的解釋是有邏輯的。

provide an explanation 提供一個說明

8　presume　[prɪˋzum]　*vt.*　假定，假設，揣測

The judge must presume innocence until he has evidence of guilt.

在罪狀未證實前，法官需假定被告無罪。

presumed sb. to be sth. 揣測某人是……

9　needful　[ˋnɪdfəl]　*adj.*　必要的，需要的

Jason donates $5000 to the needful charity.

傑森捐款五千元給需要的慈善機構。

the needful 所需

10 **conclusion** [kən`kluʒən] *n.* 結論，推論；結尾

The end of your essay is a powerful conclusion.
你的文章末段是強而有力的結論。
come to a conclusion 決定……；結果是……

11 **practically** [`præktɪk!ɪ] *adv.* 實際上；幾乎

It's practically impossible to predict when the earthquake will happen.
幾乎無法預告地震何時會發生。

12 **rave** [rev] *n.* *vi.* 熱切讚揚；狂罵；胡亂地說

The director's new film received raves in the paper.
導演的新作在報紙上受到讚揚。
rave at 狂罵
rave over / about 極力誇獎

13 **contention** [kən`tɛnʃən] *n.* 爭論，論點

It is our contention that taxes are too high.
我們的論點是課稅太重。

14 **nay** [ne] *adv.* 否，不，不但如是 *n.* 否定；反對（票、者）

Jeffrey is a yea and nay man.
傑佛瑞是一個優柔寡斷的人。
We agree, nay, we encourage it.
我們同意，不，我們鼓勵這件事。

15 **shall** [ʃæl] *v.* *aux.* （我，我們）將要

Where shall we go for lunch?

我們要去哪吃午餐？

You shall have to be careful when driving.

開車時要小心。

16 **accuse**   [ə`kjuz]   *vt.*   指責；歸咎於

Kevin often accuses nature for his own failures.

凱文常把自己的失敗歸咎於天。

accuse sb. of 指控某人……

17 **persecute**   [`pɜsɪ,kjut]   *vt.*   迫害，殘害

Jay complained of being persecuted by the press.

傑抱怨他被媒體迫害。

18 **headlong**   [`hɛd,lɔŋ]   *adj.*   *adv.*   頭向前的（地）

The boy fell headlong into the tent.

男孩一頭栽進帳篷裡。

rush / plunge headlong into sth. 一頭栽進……

19 **hypocrite**   [`hɪpəkrɪt]   *n.*   偽君子，偽善者

The book tells of an honorable man who turns out to be a hypocrite.

這本書講述一位高尚的人後來變成偽君子。

20 **debate**   [dɪ`bet]   *n.*   *vt.*   *vi.*   爭論；辯論

After a long debate, the House of Commons approved the bill.

經過長時間的辯論，下議院通過了議案。

heated / fierce debate 激烈的爭論

provoke / trigger a debate 引發爭論

21 scoff [skɔf] *vt.* *vi.* 嘲笑，嘲弄

Tony scoffed at Nancy's fear.
湯尼嘲笑南西的害怕。

22 enough [ə`nʌf] *adv.* 足夠地

Are the onions cooked enough?
這些洋蔥夠煮嗎？

lucky / unfortunate enough to do sth. ……的發生真是夠幸運或不幸

23 censure [`sɛnʃə] *n.* *vt.* *vi.* 責難，非難

Those kids were censured as liars.
那些孩子們被指責為騙子。

24 condemn [kən`dɛm] *vt.* 譴責，指責；判刑

The rule has been condemned as an attack on civil rights.
這規則被指責是對公民權的攻擊。

condemn sb. for doing sth. 因……譴責某人

25 lesson [`lɛsn] *n.* 功課，課；課程

Kate missed a lesson yesterday because she overslept.
凱特昨天因睡過頭錯過了一節課。

be good at lessons at school 在學校功課好

26 ashamed [ə`ʃemd] *adj.* 慚愧的；羞恥的

The politician is ashamed of his former dishonorable

behavior.
政客對他以前不光彩的行為感到羞愧。

27 thoughtless　[ˈθɔtlɪs]　*adj.*　欠考慮的；自私的

It's thoughtless of you to leave without informing us.
你未告知就離開是未為我們著想的。

be thoughtless of danger 不考慮危險

28 already　[ɔlˈrɛdɪ]　*adv.*　早已，已經

The train had already gone when I arrived at the station.
當我到達車站時，火車已經走了。

My son was already dressed before I woke up.
我兒子在我起床前已經穿好了衣服。

主題 2

29 conservative　[kənˈsɝvətɪv]　*adj.*　保守的　*n.*　保守的人

The Conservatives are opposed to any reformation.
保守分子反對改革。

Henry held the conservative views on education.
亨利對教育抱持守舊的觀點。

a conservative guess / estimate 保守的猜測或估計

30 fringe　[frɪndʒ]　*n.*　穗，毛邊；邊緣

Your research had only touched upon the fringe of the case.
你的研究只談到了事件的邊緣。

fringe benefit 邊際效益

主題 3

Transportation & Real Estate 交通與房地產

Vehicles 運載工具

Track 25

1 sledge　[slɛdʒ]　*n.*　雪橇，大錘

After it had stopped snowing, they all went sledging.
雪停之後，他們都去乘雪橇玩。

The puppy is on the sledge.
小狗在雪橇上。

by sledge 以雪橇

2 horseback　[`hɔrs,bæk]　*n.*　馬背

In Britain, knights would tilt on horseback.
在英國，騎士們以前常騎在馬背上比武。

The soldier on horseback is really brave.
在馬背的士兵很勇敢。

on horseback 在馬背上

3 wagon　[ˈwægən]　*n.*　敞篷馬車

The enemy attacked our wagon train and robbed everything.
敵人襲擊了我們的運貨馬車隊並搶走所有東西。

go on the wagon 戒酒
fall off the wagon 戒酒後又破戒

4 sleigh [sleɪ] *n.* 雪橇

Do you want to ride on a sleigh this afternoon?
今天下午你想要騎雪橇嗎？
a sleigh ride 一趟雪橇行

5 buggy [`bʌgɪ] *n.* 輕型馬車，嬰兒車

This mother put her little son in the buggy.
這名母親把她兒子放在嬰兒車裡。

6 carriage [`kærɪdʒ] *n.* 客車廂；四輪馬車

He ordered a carriage to come, and we drove off on it.
他安排了一輛馬車，我們則坐上馬車離開。

7 motor [`motɚ] *n.* 發動機；機動車

They work in the motor industry.
他們從事汽車工業。

8 automobile [`ɔtəmə,bil] *n.* 汽車，機動車

Linda rushed the children into the automobile.
琳達急忙地把孩子們趕進汽車裡。

9 novelty [`nɑvḷtɪ] *n.* 新穎；新奇的事物

Going to the cinema is kind of a novelty to my grandmother.
到電影院去對我祖母而言算是件新奇的事。
novelty value 新鮮的價值感
the novelty wore off 新鮮感消失
something of a novelty 新鮮的事物

10 **essential** [ɪˋsɛnʃəl] *adj.* 必要的，本質的

There are not any essential differences between the two plans.

這兩項計畫並沒有本質上的不同。

11 **masculine** [ˋmæskjəlɪn] *adj.* 男性的；強壯的

Our new manager is a young woman who is sort of masculine looking.

我們新來的經理是一名年輕女性，看起來卻有點男性化。

12 **truck** [trʌk] *n.* 卡車

Look out! There's a truck coming!

注意！有輛卡車過來了！

13 **pavement** [ˋpevmənt] *n.* （英）人行道

Kelly dropped my camera on the pavement and broke it.

凱莉把我的照相機掉在人行道上摔壞了。

14 **sidewalk** [ˋsaɪd͵wɔk] *n.* 人行道

We cannot throw away any garbage on the sidewalk.

我們不可以在人行道上丟垃圾。

sidewalk artist 街頭藝術家

15 **bike** [baɪk] *n.* 自行車

I want to go for a bike ride in the afternoon.

我下午想去騎腳踏車。

16 helmet [ˋhɛlmɪt] *n.* 頭盔，鋼盔

Wearing a helmet can protect your head.
戴頭盔可以保護你的頭部。
crash helmet 全罩式安全帽

17 license [ˋlaɪsns] *n.* 許可；執照 *vt.* 准許

Right at the age of 18, Erica took out a driving license.
一到十八歲，艾莉卡就拿到駕駛執照了。
a license to do sth. 可以做某事的執照

18 gasoline [ˋgæsə͵lin] *n.* （美）汽油

How often do you have to fill up your car with gasoline?
你多久要加油一次？
unleaded gasoline 無鉛汽油

主題 3

19 fuel [ˋfjʊəl] *n.* 燃料 *vt.* 給……加燃料

There was something wrong with the fuel lines, so the missile did not blast off.
燃料管路出了些問題，所以導彈沒有發射。
save fuel 節省能源

20 cylinder [ˋsɪlɪndɚ] *n.* 圓筒；圓柱；汽缸

There is too much gas and not enough air in the cylinder.
汽缸裡汽油太多而空氣不足。
be working / firing on all cylinders 全力工作；全速運行

21 **tyre**　[taɪr]　*n.*　輪胎，車胎

A nail is sticking in the tyre, and the tyre is getting flat.

輪胎上插著一根釘子，漸漸沒氣了。

22 **brake**　[brek]　*n.*　閘，煞車　*vi.*　制動

If the brake doesn't grip properly, it is very dangerous to hit the road.

如果煞車不靈，上路是很危險的。

23 **squeak**　[skwik]　*vi.*　尖叫

The boy squeaked nervously and started to cry.

這男孩緊張地尖叫，並開始哭泣。

24 **failing**　[ˋfelɪŋ]　*n.*　失敗，缺點，過失

Jenny knows very well about her failings.

珍妮很清楚自己的缺點。

a human failing 人性弱點

25 **defect**　[dɪˋfɛkt]　*n.*　缺點，缺陷

The young man in our department has a speech defect.

我們部門的那個年輕人有語言缺陷。

a genetic defect 基因缺陷

26 **defective**　[dɪˋfɛktɪv]　*adj.*　有缺陷的，欠缺的

We need to call back all the defective products that have already been sent out.

我們必須回收已經出貨的瑕疵產品。

27 gear [gɪr] *n.* 齒輪傳動裝置;(汽車的)排檔

Does your car have three or four gears?

你的車是三檔還是四檔?

get into gear 開始著手

out of gear 失去控制

change gears 換檔/改變作法

28 reverse [rɪˋvɝs] *vt.* 顛倒,翻轉 *n.* 背面

Nancy's position and mine are now reversed, and I became her supervisor.

南茜和我的位置現在倒轉過來了,我變成了她的上司。

reverse oneself 改變想法

reverse roles / positions 角色互換

主題 3

29 forward [ˋfɔrwəd] *adv.* 向前

The guard hurried forward to meet the princess.

守衛趕緊走上前去迎接公主。

going forward 在未來

go forward to 晉級

30 auto [ˋɔto] *n.* (口語)汽車

The auto workers took to the streets for higher pay.

汽車工人為爭取提高工資而走上街頭。

Unit 02　Public Transport 公共運輸

Track 26

1　conveyance　[kən`veəns]　*n.*　運輸，運輸工具，財產讓與

We don't allow wheeled conveyances of any kind in our garden.

我們的花園不准任何輪子的交通工具。

2　metropolis　[mə`trɑplɪs]　*n.*　大城市

My city has become a busy metropolis.

我住的城市已經成為一個大都會。

3　alteration　[ˌɔltə`reʃən]　*n.*　變更；改變

The schedule of our event is subject to alteration.

我們的活動時程有可能更改。

4　renovation　[ˌrɛnə`veʃən]　*n.*　革新，翻新

The entire church needs renovation, and it will take a long time.

這座教堂需要維修翻新，而且耗時不短。

in need of renovation 需要翻新

5　elaborate　[ɪ`læbə‚ret]　*adj.*　複雜的；精心製作的

They made elaborate props for the play.

他們為這齣戲精心製作道具。

There will be guests in our house this evening, so my mother has prepared an elaborate dinner.
今晚我們家有客人，所以媽媽準備了很精美的晚餐。

6 project [prəˋdʒɛkt] *n.* 方案，工程 *vi.* 伸出

They will complete the project to establish a new national park next spring.
他們明年春天將完成建造新的國家公園工程。

a project to do sth. 做某事計畫

do a project on sth. 針對某事做一個方案

7 feat [fit] *n.* 功績，壯舉

The player won three consecutive championships and that was really a feat.
這名選手連續贏得三座冠軍，而這真是個功績。

a feat of engineering 工程上的壯舉

no mean feat 很困難的事

perform / achieve / accomplish a feat 達到壯舉

主題 3

8 commotion [kəˋmoʃən] *n.* 騷動，動亂

That young girl is always making a great commotion about nothing.
那名年輕女孩總是無理取鬧。

cause a commotion 造成騷動

9 excursion [ɪkˋskɝʒən] *n.* 遠足旅行

Let's discuss our excursion next summer.
我們來討論明年夏天的遠足旅行吧。

on an excursion 在遠足旅行中

10 **frequent**　[`frikwənt]　*adj.*　時常發生的；經常的

The plant is in frequent need of raw materials.

這座工廠經常原料不足。

11 **interval**　[`ɪntəvl̩]　*n.*　間隔；休息；間距

Vehicles should maintain the proper intervals between each other.

車輛彼此之間應保持適當的間距。

at regular intervals 在規律的間隔之下

interval between… 在……之間的交替

12 **inconvenience**　[ˌɪnkən`vinjəns]　*n.*　不便，困難

I don't care. It's just a minor inconvenience.

我不介意，這只是一點小不方便而已。

13 **uncomfortable**　[ʌn`kʌmfətəbl̩]　*adj.*　不舒服的；不自在的

Stop looking at her! That is making her uncomfortable.

別再看她了！那讓她覺得很不舒服。

14 **mingle**　[`mɪŋgl̩]　*vt.*　使混合　*vi.*　混合起來

The undercover agent mingled in the crowd and lost in sight.

這名臥底探員或入人群中失去蹤影了。

15 **throng**　[θrɔŋ]　*n.*　群，人群　*vt.*　擠滿

The local airport was thronged with vacationers from

overseas.

本地機場擠滿了外國來的度假客。

a throng of loud tourists 一群說話大聲的遊客

throng to do sth. 擠著去做某事

16 **capacity**   [kə`pæsətɪ]   *n.*   容量；能力；能量

Do you believe in equality of capacity? Well, I believe in equality of opportunity.

你相信能力均等嗎？我相信機會均等。

work at full capacity 全力工作

17 **passage**   [`pæsɪdʒ]   *n.*   通過；通路，通道

The lane is too narrow to allow the passage of two cars at the same time.

這條巷子太窄，不能容許兩輛車同時通過。

the passage of time 時間流逝

18 **jerk**   [dʒɝk]   *vt.*   猛地一拉   *vi.*   急拉

The bus jerked to a stop, and many people lost their balance.

公車晃動幾下停住了，許多人失去了平衡。

19 **swift**   [swɪft]   *adj.*   快的；反應快的

When we knew the flight was canceled, we were swift to find another airline.

當我們得知班機取消時，我們很快地找到另一家航空公司。

sb. is not too swift 某人不太聰明

主題 3

20 rather [ˋræðɚ] *adv.* 寧可，寧願；相當

I'd rather walk to work than take a bus.
我寧可走路上班，也不要搭公車。

21 alternate [ˋɔltɚ͵nɪt] *vt.* 使交替　*adj.* 交替的

That woman alternated between anger and sadness.
那個女人一下生氣一下傷心。

22 highway [ˋhaɪ͵we] *n.* 公路；大路

After the highway was completed, the business of this town declined.
這條新公路完成之後，這個小鎮的生意一落千丈。

highway robbery 被敲竹槓
my way or the highway 同意我，不然就走

23 accident [ˋæksədənt] *n.* 意外；事故

We are all shocked to hear about her accident.
我們聽到她的意外都感到驚嚇。

24 dispatch [dɪˋspætʃ] *vt.* 派遣；調度　*n.* 急件

The journalist dispatched the report to her newspaper.
這名記者把報導發送到她的報社。

The boss dispatched a young boy to fetch the documents.
老闆派一名年輕男孩去拿回文件。

with dispatch 快而有效率地

25 ordinary [ˋɔrdn͵ɛrɪ] *adj.* 平常的；平凡的

You have to complete the job in an ordinary way.

你必須用一般的方式完成這份工作。

This book described the way of life of the ordinary people in Australia.

這本書描繪了澳洲人平常的生活方式。

out of the ordinary 不尋常地

26 safety   [`seftɪ]   *n.*   安全，保險

The new car design put together the latest safety features.

新的汽車設計備有最新安全措施的特點。

27 inspection   [ɪn`spɛkʃən]   *n.*   檢查，審查；檢閱

All the students were lined up for the inspection.

所有的學生排好隊接受檢閱。

主題 **3**

28 inspector   [ɪn`spɛktɚ]   *n.*   檢查員；巡官

The school inspector is coming to our school next month.

督學下個月要來我們學校視察。

29 cheery   [`tʃɪrɪ]   *adj.*   愉快的

The superstar gave us a cheery greeting, and he was really friendly.

那名巨星愉快地跟我們打招呼，而他真的很友善。

30 amiable   [`emɪəb!]   *adj.*   和藹的，親切的

The people in our neighborhood are all amiable.

我們社區裡的人都很和藹可親。

amiable tone of voice 親切的語調

Unit 03　Traffic 交通

Track 27

1 gutter [ˋgʌtɚ] *n.* 溝，邊溝；簷槽

The gutters are blocked, and it will become terrible when a typhoon comes.

排水溝堵住了，颱風來的話會很糟糕。

2 irregular [ɪˋrɛgjələ] *adj.* 不規則的；不整齊的

He lives in an irregular life, and that is not healthy.

他過著不規律的生活，而那很不健康。

3 bump [bʌmp] *vt.　vi.* 碰，撞；撞擊

She got a bump on her forehead, and it looked like it hurt.

她額頭上撞起了一個包，看起來很痛。

4 obstacle [ˋɑbstəkl] *n.* 障礙，障礙物，妨害

He has overcome many obstacles and finally become a successful businessman.

他克服了很多障礙，而最後成為一位成功的生意人。

obstacle to sth. 某事物的障礙

remove an obstacle 除去障礙

5 barrier [ˋbærɪr] *n.* 柵欄，屏障；障礙

The runner jumped over the barrier.
跑者跳躍過柵欄。

barrier to sth. 某事物的障礙

barrier between ⋯⋯之間的障礙

language barrier 語言障礙

6　access　[`æksɛs]　*n.*　接近；通道，入口

The only access to their beach house is along that dark road.
只有沿著那條狹窄的路走才能到達他們的房子。

7　interchange　[͵ɪntɚ`tʃendʒ]　*n.*　立體交叉道，互換

Leave the highway at the next interchange.
在下個交流道下高速公路。

interchange of ideas 意見交流

8　tedious　[`tidɪəs]　*adj.*　冗長乏味的，沉悶的

The tedious story really made me feel sleepy.
這個冗長乏味的故事真的令我好想睡覺。

tedious details 冗長的細節

9　horrid　[`hɔrɪd]　*adj.*　可怕的；極可厭的；毛骨悚然的

Don't be so horrid to your sister!
別對你妹妹那麼壞！

10　abominable　[ə`bɑmənəb!]　*adj.*　可厭的，天氣極壞的

The coffee at that shop is abominable.
那家店的咖啡超難喝的。

abominable snowman 雪怪

11 **snarl** [snɑrl] *n.* *v.* 糾纏，混亂

Peter was caught in the traffic snarls this morning.

彼得今天早上被困在交通大混亂中。

snarl up 使困在交通中

12 **blockade** [blɑ`ked] *n.* *v.* 封鎖

The economic blockade is making that country poorer and poorer.

經濟封鎖使得那個國家愈來愈貧窮。

impose / lift a blockade 實施／解除封鎖

13 **dwindle** [`dwɪndl] *v.* 日漸減少，變小

A severe drought dwindled the crops and made farmers worried.

一場嚴重的乾旱使農作物歉收，並讓農夫感到憂心。

【同】decrease, diminish, lessen

【反】swell, expand, augment

14 **abate** [ə`bet] *v.* 減輕，降低

No matter what you say, you can't abate his anger.

無論你說什麼都無法平息他的憤怒。

abate pollution 減輕汙染

15 **prudence** [`prudns] *n.* 謹慎，小心

Andy lacks financial prudence and has lost a lot of money.

安迪缺乏謹慎理財的觀念，已經賠掉好多錢了。

with prudence 小心地；謹慎地

16 prudent [`prudnt] *adj.* 謹慎的；精明的

Rebecca is a prudent manager, and we all count on her.

瑞貝卡是一位謹慎的經理，我們都很仰賴她。

17 fasten [`fæsn] *vt. vi.* 紮牢；扣住

I asked Stacy to fasten the notice to the board.

我請史黛西把通知貼到佈告板上。

18 attentive [ə`tɛntɪv] *adj.* 注意的；有禮貌的

We should be attentive to what our parents say.

我們應該注意父母所說的話。

attentive to 注意

19 irritate [`ɪrə,tet] *vt.* 激怒；引起不愉快

It really irritates me when I see my brother doing nothing but watch TV and eat.

看到我弟弟無所事事，只會看電視和吃東西，真讓我抓狂。

irritate sensitive skin 刺激敏感性皮膚

【同】annoy, bother, harass

20 constrain [kən`stren] *vt.* 強迫；壓制，抑制

Lack of money constrained our project.

缺乏金錢壓制了我們的計畫。

constrain sb. to do sth. 強迫某人不准做某事

21 **enrage**　[ɪnˋredʒ]　*vt.*　激怒，使暴怒

The gentleman was enraged by her childish behavior.

這位紳士被她幼稚的行為給激怒。

The coverage of that journalist enraged many people.

那位記者的報導激怒了很多人。

be enraged at 對……感到生氣

22 **incident**　[ˋɪnsədnt]　*n.*　小事件；插曲；事變

Every one of us couldn't forget the incident at the camp last summer.

我們所有人都無法忘記去年在營地發生的事件。

without incident 沒有插曲地；順利地

【同】occurance, affair, event

23 **scramble**　[ˋskræmbl]　*vi.*　*n.*　爬行，攀登

It's still a scramble from here to get to the top of the hill.

從這裡往上爬到山頂還有一大段路呢。

scramble to one's feet 慌張地站起來

【同】climb, scale, crawl

24 **thither**　[ˋθɪðɚ]　*adj.*　對岸的，那邊的

The innocent girl ran hither and thither in the garden.

純真的女孩在乎花園裡亂跑。

hither and thither 到處

25 **hoot**　[hut]　*n.*　叫囂，嘲罵聲，鳴響

There is an accident right in front. It's of no use keeping

hooting.

前面有車禍，一直按喇叭也沒有用。

hoot with laughter 邊笑邊叫

hoot in disgust 因討厭而叫罵

26 **warning**　[ˋwɔrnɪŋ]　*n.*　警告，告誡，鑒誡

The red light is a warning sign for stop.

紅燈是警告停止前進的信號。

27 **rash**　[ræʃ]　*adj.*　輕率的；魯莽的

It is rash to say you don't like someone before you really get to know him.

在你真的了解某人之前，說你不喜歡人家是很魯莽的。

rash decision 魯莽的決定

28 **gesture**　[ˋdʒɛstʃə]　*n.*　姿勢，手勢；姿態

The defeated enemy raised their hands in a gesture of despair.

戰敗的敵人舉起雙手以表示絕望。

make a gesture 做手勢

29 **cope**　[kop]　*vi.*　對付，應付

Melissa is very good at coping with any difficult situation.

梅麗莎非常善於應付任何困難的情況。

30 **smog**　[smɑg]　*n.*　煙霧

There is smog in the air, so the air quality is very bad.

空氣中都是煙霧，所以空氣品質非常糟。

Unit 04

Air 航空

Track 28

1 aircraft [ˋɛr͵kræft] *n.* 飛機，飛行器

This airfield cannot allow a large passenger aircraft to land.

這個機場無法讓大型民航班機降落。

2 jet [dʒɛt] *n.* 噴射；噴氣發動機

Jet propulsion can make aircraft fly.

噴氣推進可以使飛機飛起來。

【同】spray, spurt, gush

3 charter [ˋtʃɑrtɚ] *vt.* 租 *n.* 憲章；契據

The flight is for charter, so we cannot book a seat by ourselves.

這架航班是包機，所以我們無法自己訂位。

4 venture [ˋvɛntʃɚ] *n.* *vi.* 冒險 *vt.* 敢於

Nothing ventured, nothing gained.

【諺】不入虎穴，焉得虎子

joint venture 合作投資案

5 somewhere [ˋsʌm͵hwɛr] *adv.* 在某處 *n.* 某地

You can find the text somewhere in the Bible.

你會在聖經裡找到這段文字。

6 wherever [hwɛrˋɛvɚ] *adv.* 無論在（到）哪裡

You may sit wherever you like.

你隨便想坐哪兒都行。

or wherever 或任何其他地方

7 confirmation [ˌkɑnfɚˋmeʃən] *n.* 證實；確定；確認

Remember to send a confirmation to the hotel before you leave for your destination.

在出發到目的地之前，記得向飯店寄出確認。

official confirmation 官方確認

8 embark [ɪmˋbɑrk] *vi.* 乘船；著手；從事；上飛機

We embarked for Green Island in the afternoon.

我們下午乘船去綠島。

embark on 開始做

【同】board

9 move [muv] *n.* 行動，步驟

The ballerina's every move was graceful and beautiful.

這個芭蕾舞女伶的每一個動作都很優雅美麗。

on the move 很忙碌／旅行中

10 departure [dɪˋpɑrtʃɚ] *n.* 離開，出發，起程

The girl's arrival coincided with our departure.

這個女孩來到時我們正好離開。

主題 3

departure for 前往，離開

departure from 背離

11 launch [lɔntʃ] *vt.* 發射；發動（戰爭等）

The country has successfully launched a man-made satellite.

那個國家成功地發射了一顆人造衛星。

launch into 開始做某事

launch out 開始於做些冒險的事，出海

12 east [ist] *adv.* 向東方；往東邊　*n.* 東方

He traveled east.

他向東旅行。

13 altitude [ˋæltəˌtjud] *n.* 高度；高處

There are often strong winds at this altitude.

在這種高度經常有強風。

【同】height

14 elevation [ˌɛləˋveʃən] *n.* 高度；標高；隆腫

At higher elevations, it is very cold.

在較高的地方，天氣很冷。

an elevation of 在……高的地方

15 height [haɪt] *n.* 高，高度；高處

The strange man was about five feet in height.

那個陌生男子的身高大約 5 英尺。

at the height of one's success 在成功的巔峰

---

at the height of stupidity 在愚蠢的極致

16 lofty [ˋlɔftɪ] *adj.* 高聳的；高尚的

When we got to the mountain top, we stood in awe of the lofty trees.
當我們抵達山頂時，高聳入雲的大樹令我們驚歎不已。
lofty mountains 高山
lofty ambitions 崇高抱負
lofty manner 自負的態度

17 hover [ˋhʌvɚ] *vi.* 徘徊；彷徨；翱翔

The hawk is hovering in the sky.
鷹在天空盤旋。
hover around 盤旋

18 mid [mɪd] *adj.* 中間的，中央的，中部的

The breaking news was that two planes collided in mid air.
最新消息是有兩架飛機在半空中相撞。

19 thrill [θrɪl] *vt.* *vi.* （使）激動

The sight of the sunset thrilled me, and I was speechless.
日落的景色讓我激動不已，而且說不出話來。
thrill to 因……而激動
thrills and spills 刺激的部分
the thrill of the chase 追求的刺激感

20 envious [ˋɛnvɪəs] *adj.* 嫉妒的，羨慕的

主題 3

We should not be envious of others' success.
我們不該嫉妒別人的成功。
envious looks 羨慕的眼神

21 **steer**　[stɪr]　*vt.*　*vi.*　駕駛

Her boyfriend steered the car skillfully through the narrow lanes.
她的男朋友熟練地駕駛著汽車穿過狹窄的巷弄。

22 **craft**　[kræft]　*n.*　工藝；手藝，行業

These people are trying to use modern techniques to enhance this traditional craft.
這群人試圖利用現代技術以提升這項傳統工業。
art and crafts 藝術與工藝
the writer's craft 寫作的技巧

23 **skill**　[`skɪl]　*n.*　技能；技巧；熟練

The crisis is pretty much a test of his courage and skill.
這次危難對他的勇氣和技能是一個考驗。

24 **drone**　[dron]　*v.*　嗡嗡地響　*n.*　單調的低音

There is an airplane droning low in the sky.
有一架飛機在低空中嗡嗡飛過。
You can hear the distant drone of traffic from this flat.
從這間公寓可以聽到遠處的交通聲音。

25 **radar**　[`redɑr]　*n.*　雷達，無線電探測器

After five days, they finally found the yacht on their radar screen.

五天後，他們終於在雷達屏上看到了那艘遊艇。
below / under the radar 沒有被發現
on / off the radar screen 專注／不專注

26 overhead　[`ovə`hɛd]　*adv.*　在頭上；在空中

My mother stores all kinds of snacks in the overhead cabinet.
我媽媽把各式各樣的零食收在頭上的櫃子裡。
When we lay on the beach, a helicopter flew overhead.
當我們躺在沙灘時，有一架直升機在空中飛過。

27 carrier　[`kærɪə]　*n.*　運輸公司

My company has been working with that carrier for a long time.
我的公司跟那家運輸業者合作很久了。

28 object　[`abdʒɪkt]　*n.*　物，物體；目的

There are various objects that were on the table in the living room.
客廳的桌子上擺著各種各樣的物體。

29 parcel　[`pars!]　*n.*　包裹

Helen tied the parcel carefully with twine because it was her best friend's birthday present.
海倫用細繩仔細地來捆紮包裹，因為這是她最好朋友的生日禮物。

30 package　[`pækɪdʒ]　*n.*　包裹；包裝

My cousin in France sent me a package by post.
我在法國的表哥郵寄給我一個包裹。

主題 3

Rail 鐵路

Track 29

1 pilgrimage [`pɪlgrəmɪdʒ] *n.* 朝聖之旅

Every year, many people make pilgrimages to Mozart's birthplace.

每年有很多人去莫札特的出生地朝聖。

go on / make a pilgrimage 參加朝聖

place of pilgrimage 朝聖地

2 sojourn [so`dʒɝn] *n. v.* 逗留，寄居

Sophie sojourned with a friend in London for three weeks.

蘇菲在倫敦一個朋友的住處待了三個星期。

a sojourn in 在某地短暫停留

3 railroad [`rel,rod] *n.* 鐵路 *vi.* 由鐵路運輸

We can enjoy free transportation for a certain amount of baggage if we use the railroad.

如果我們使用鐵路，可以享有一定數量的行李免費運送。

4 railway [`rel,we] *n.* 鐵路，鐵道

It is interesting to see the railway lines running parallel to the road while driving.

開車時，看到鐵路線和道路平行是很有趣的。

5 rugged　　[ˋrʌgɪd]　　*adj.*　　崎嶇不平的；堅固耐用的；堅毅的

The path to glory is always rugged.

【諺】通向光榮的道路常常是崎嶇的。

6 rust　　[rʌst]　　*n.*　　鏽　　*vi.*　　生鏽，氧化

The metal on your bag has corroded away because of rust.

你手提包上的金屬已經因為生鏽而腐蝕。

covered with rust 佈滿了鏽

rust away 生鏽而漸漸腐蝕

7 rusty　　[ˋrʌstɪ]　　*adj.*　　生鏽的；變遲鈍的

My uncle's collection of spoons has become rusty from disuse.

我舅舅的湯匙收集品因沒用而生鏽了。

After graduating from college, my French is a little rusty.

從大學畢業之後，我的法文就有點不流利了。

主題 3

8 track　　[træk]　　*n.*　　足跡；（火車的）軌道

I heard the news on TV saying that a train jumped the track.

我聽到電視新聞說有輛火車出軌了。

9 rail　　[rel]　　*n.*　　鐵軌；軌道；鐵路

Shipping goods by road is usually cheaper than by rail.

公路運送貨物通常比鐵路運輸便宜。

rail transportation 鐵路運輸

10 **horizontal** [ˌhɑrəˈzɑnt!] *adj.* 地平的；水準的

Remember to keep the patient in a horizontal position with his feet raised a little.

記得保持病人水平躺著，腳有點抬高。

11 **parallel** [ˈpærəˌlɛl] *adj.* 平行的；相同的

They are like two parallel lines and never have anything in common.

他們像是兩條平行線一樣，從來沒有任何共通之處。

parallel to / with 和……平行；相似

12 **punctual** [ˈpʌŋktʃʊəl] *adj.* 嚴守時刻的；準時的

We all arrive on time because the host liked his guests to be punctual.

因為這個主人家喜歡他的客人守時，所以我們全都準時到達。

a punctual start 準時開始

punctual payment 準時付款

13 **timetable** [ˈtaɪmˌteb!] *n.* 時間表，時刻表

Can anyone think of a better timetable that suits everyone?

有人能想出更好的時間表，適合每個人嗎？

14 **platform** [ˈplætˌfɔrm] *n.* 月台；平台；講台

Sometimes you need to get a ticket to the platform even though you are not taking a train but just seeing your friends off.

有時候你要買票才能到月台，雖然你並沒有要搭火車，而只是去替朋友送行而已。

15 **alight**　[ə`laɪt]　*vi.*　落下，偶然發現

When the bus stopped in front of the department store, almost every passenger alighted.
當公車停在百貨公司前，幾乎每個人都下車了。
alight on 降落在
alight from 從……下車
alight on an idea 想到一個主意

16 **worldly**　[`wɝldlɪ]　*adj.*　世間的，世俗的，世上的

That politician had a mind for worldly reputation.
那位政治人物希望得到世間的名聲。
worldly success 世俗的成功
worldly goods / possessions 個人的所有財產
worldly-wise 歷練豐富的

主題 3

17 **station**　[`steʃən]　*vt.*　駐紮；安置　*n.*　車站

There are two guards stationed at the gate in order to protect the prince.
為了保護王子，門口有兩名警衛站崗。

18 **depot**　[`dipo]　*n.*　貨棧；倉庫

The depot by the harbor was destroyed by the typhoon.
港口附近的倉庫被颱風摧毀了。
an arms depot 軍火庫
distribution depot 發貨倉庫

19 **locomotive**　[ˌlokə`motɪv]　*adj.*　運動的　*n.*　火車

A locomotive is actually a railway engine.

火車頭其實就是火車引擎。

20 wheel [hwil] *n.* 輪，車輪

A bicycle has two wheels.

自行車有兩個輪子。

21 spin [spɪn] *vt.* 紡；使旋轉 *n.* 旋轉

The pitcher spun and threw the ball; it was a hard technique.

投手投球時讓球旋轉，那是一項困難的技巧。

spin a tale 編故事

22 service [ˋsɝvɪs] *n.* 服務

I think you should seek the services of a lawyer.

我認為你應該尋求律師的服務。

23 consign [kənˋsaɪn] *v.* 托運，托人看管

Please be informed that the goods of your order have been consigned by railway.

請注意您所訂購的貨物已由鐵路託運。

consign sb. / sth. to 把某人或某物交給……

24 haul [hɔl] *vt.* 拖曳；拖運

It's a haul of twenty miles from here to your town.

從這裡到你的城鎮，那可是二十英里路程的搬運。

haul oneself out of bed 勉強起床

haul away 帶走

a long haul 困難的任務

25 cargo [`kɑrgo] *n.* 船貨，貨物

The great ship can carry a cargo of 1,000 tons.

這艘大船能載一千噸重的貨物。

26 goods [gʊdz] *n.* 商品；貨物

The store sells many kinds of goods, and you should take a look.

那家商店販賣很多種類的商品，你應該要看一看。

27 bulk [bʌlk] *n.* 物體，容積，大批

It is usually cheaper if you buy things in bulk.

大量買進商品通常會比較便宜。

28 strap [stræp] *n.* 帶子 *vt.* 捆紮

Before you check in your baggage, make sure you have strapped it up.

在你托運行李之前，要確認已經把行李捆綁好了。

29 tow [to] *vt. n.* 拖引；牽引

Our car broke down in the rain, so we had to tow it to the nearest garage.

我們的車子在大雨中拋錨，所以我們必須把車子拖到最近的修車廠。

30 rear [rɪr] *n.* 後部，後面；背面

The piece of woodland to the rear of the house is vast.

房子後面的一片林地很廣闊。

主題 3

Unit
06

Water 水路

Track 30

1 canoe [kə`nu] *n.* 獨木舟　*vt.* 划獨木舟

These young people are canoeing in the lake.
這群年輕人在湖中划獨木舟。

My friends are going to cross the river by canoe.
我朋友要搭獨木舟渡河。

go canoeing 去划獨木舟

paddle your own canoe【英】靠你自己

2 barge [bɑrdʒ] *n.* 駁船；大型遊船

The barge on the river is very big.
河中的駁船好大一艘。

barge in on 打擾

3 tug [tʌg] *vt.* 拖拉；牽引　*n.* 拖曳艇

After we had a fight, my girlfriend tried to tug my hand away.
在吵架之後，我的女朋友試圖把我的手拉開。

tug at sb.'s heartstrings 牽動某人的心弦

tug of love（離婚夫妻）為子女爭執

4 steamer [`stimɚ] *n.* 輪船，汽船

We need to get on the steamer leaving for New York.

我們必須搭上前往紐約的輪船。

5 steamship [ˋstim͵ʃɪp] *n.* 汽船，輪船

Some passengers are chatting on the deck of the steamship.

有些旅客在這艘輪船的甲板上聊天。

6 steamboat [ˋstim͵bot] *n.* 汽船，輪船

The couple traveled on the steamboat along the east coast.

這對情侶坐著汽船沿著東海岸旅行。

by steamboat 搭輪船

7 afloat [əˋflot] *adj.* *adv.* 漂浮著（的）

The fisherman set the boat afloat.

漁夫讓船浮到水面上。

keep a business afloat 讓生意勉強撐過去

stay afloat 勉強撐得過去

8 escort [ˋɛskɔrt] *n.* *vt.* 護衛，護送

After the party, John escorted his girlfriend home.

派對之後，約翰護送他的女朋友回家。

9 fleet [flit] *n.* 艦隊；船隊；車隊

The fleet is carrying out a maneuver in the Pacific Ocean.

該艦隊正在太平洋進行演習。

10 rove [rov] *v.* 流浪，漂泊

He has decided to rove the country for one year.

主題 3

他決定要漫遊全國一年。

rove over / around（眼神）飄移

11 **anchor**　[ˋæŋkɚ]　*n.*　錨　*vi.*　拋錨，停泊

Several boats dropped anchor at a harbor.

港灣裡停泊著幾艘船。

at anchor 停泊中

12 **lighthouse**　[ˋlaɪt͵haʊs]　*n.*　燈塔

There is always a lighthouse at a harbor.

港口一定都會有燈塔。

in the lighthouse 在燈塔裡

13 **navigable**　[ˋnævəɡəb!]　*adj.*　可航行的；適於航行的

The government is building a canal that is navigable all the year.

政府正在興建一座可以全年通航的運河。

14 **gulf**　[ɡʌlf]　*n.*　海灣；鴻溝

We live near a gulf that extends northward.

我們住在一個像北方延伸的海灣附近。

15 **strait**　[stret]　*n.*　海峽

While they were crossing the straits, the weather suddenly became very bad.

當他們要渡過海峽時，天氣突然變糟了。

in dire straits 在艱難的困境中

16 **canal**　[kəˋnæl]　*n.*　運河

The canal is finally open to shipping.
該運河終於通航了。

17 **tributary**　[ˋtrɪbjəˌtɛrɪ]　*n.*　*adj.*　支流（的），附屬（的）

When you reach the end of this road, you will find a tributary.
當你抵達這條路的盡頭，你會發現一條岔路。
a tributary stream 支流

18 **isle**　[aɪl]　*n.*　島；小島

The British Isles is a geographic name.
不列顛群島是一個地理名稱。

19 **pier**　[pɪr]　*n.*　（橋）墩；碼頭

We love to take a walk along the wooden pier after dinner.
晚餐後，我們喜歡沿著木製碼頭散步。

20 **pillar**　[ˋpɪlə]　*n.*　柱，柱子；棟樑

Those marble pillars in the church are really beautiful.
教堂裡的那些大理石柱真是漂亮。
a pillar of strength 支持的力量
a pillar of society 社會的中流砥柱
be driven / pushed from pillar to post 到處碰壁

21 **helm**　[hɛlm]　*n.*　舵，駕駛盤

The helm of the ship seems broken, and we need to find someone to fix it.

船上的舵好像壞掉了，我們要找人來修理。

at the helm 掌舵／掌權

take the helm 掌舵／掌權

22 stern　[stɝn]　*n.*　船尾　*adj.*　嚴厲的

The boy was sitting in the stern of the boat and soaking his feet in the river.

那個小男孩坐在船尾，把腳泡進河水裡。

When the father put on a stern face, Peter stopped talking immediately.

當爸爸的臉色變得嚴厲，彼得立刻停止說話。

23 deck　[dɛk]　*n.*　甲板

Rich people usually stay at the upper deck of a ship.

有錢人通常住在上層甲板。

hit the deck 閃避危險

clear the decks 準備行動

24 scrub　[skrʌb]　*n.*　*vt.*　擦洗，擦淨

We helped our mother scrub the floor really hard.

我們幫忙媽媽好好地擦洗地板。

25 mariner　[ˋmærənɚ]　*n.*　水手，海員

There are over 60 mariners on this ship.

船上有六十多名水手。

26 courageous [kə`redʒəs] *adj.* 勇敢的，無畏的

I think this is a very courageous action.

我覺得這是一個很有勇氣的行動。

get up the courage 提起勇氣

27 withstand [wɪð`stænd] *vt.* 抵擋，反抗

We could not withstand the fierce attack of the enemy army.

我們無法抵擋敵軍猛烈的攻擊。

withstand the test of time 經過時間的考驗

28 adverse [æd`vɝs] *adj.* 反面的，不友好的

We failed to advance because of the adverse winds.

因為逆風，所以我們無法前進。

主題 3

29 distress [dɪ`strɛs] *n.* 憂慮，悲傷；不幸

I can see the distress in Tracy's eyes, but I don't know what to say.

我可以看見崔西眼中的悲傷，但我不知道該說些什麼。

in distress 在困境中

30 peril [`pɛrəl] *n.* 危機；危險的事物

The ship was in imminent peril, and all the passengers had to get on to a lifeboat.

那條船有立即的危險，所有的乘客都必須坐上救生艇。

in grave / great / serious peril 在嚴重的危險中

fraught with peril 充滿危險

Property 財產

Track 31

1 lodging [`lɑdʒɪŋ] *n.* 寄宿，住宿；住所

I find lodgings on First Avenue.
我在第一大街上找到住宿的地方。

2 accommodation [ə,kɑmə`deʃən] *n.* 適應；和解；住處

We called the hotel for accommodations tonight.
我們打電話給旅館訂今晚的房間。

student accommodation 學生住宿

3 dwelling [`dwɛlɪŋ] *n.* 住處；寓所

The host said, "Welcome to my humble dwelling!"
主人說：「歡迎到寒舍來！」

4 cottage [`kɑtɪdʒ] *n.* 村舍；小屋

Mark has a house in Spain and a cottage near the sea.
馬克在西班牙有一棟房子，在海邊還有一間小屋。

5 homestead [`hom,stɛd] *n.* 家園；田產

We must protect our homestead.
我們必須保護我們的家園。

6 estate　[ɪs`tet]　*n.*　房地產；財產；產業

She is a real estate agent.

她是一個地產經紀人。

7 grange　[grendʒ]　*n.*　農場；農莊

They will spend their summer vacation in their aunt's grange.

他們會去他們姑姑的農莊過暑假。

They are going to buy the old grange and turn it into a villa.

他們將買下這座農莊，把它變為度假別墅。

8 squire　[skwaɪr]　*n.*　鄉紳；大地主；地方法官

The squire owned most of the land around a country village near Scotland.

這大地主擁有蘇格蘭附近一個鄉下村莊的大部分土地。

主題 3

9 immense　[ɪ`mɛns]　*adj.*　巨大的；極好的

The scientists spend an immense amount of time on the experiment.

科學家們在這個實驗花了大量的時間。

immense wealth 巨大的財富

immense value 無價

a factor of immense importance 重要的因素

10 wide　[waɪd]　*adj.*　寬廣的　*adv.*　廣闊地；充分地

The drunken man was wide awake.

酒醉的男人完全清醒了。

11 **undisturbed**　[ˌʌndɪˈstɝbd]　*adj.*　安靜的；鎮定的

Robert was undisturbed by her intimidation.

羅伯在她的恐嚇下仍鎮定。

remain undisturbed 維持安靜

12 **acre**　[ˈekɚ]　*n.*　英畝；地產

My grandpa owns one hundred acres of farmland in Australia.

我祖父在澳洲擁有一百英畝的農地。

13 **vicinity**　[vəˈsɪnətɪ]　*n.*　附近地區；近鄰

My stolen motorcycle was found in the vicinity of the train station.

我失竊的腳踏車在火車站附近找到。

14 **fruitless**　[ˈfrutlɪs]　*adj.*　無結果的

Kevin's fight with misfortune is fruitless.

凱文與厄運的對抗是徒勞無功的。

a fruitless attempt 無效的嘗試

15 **tract**　[trækt]　*n.*　大片（土地）；傳單；小冊子

The 30-acre tract will be reclaimed for a new airport.

這三十英畝土地將被開發為新機場。

The government published a tract on the damages of smoking.

政府發行一本抽菸危害的小冊子。

16 vacancy　[ˋvekənsɪ]　*n.*　空白；空缺

We have a vacancy for a secretary.
我們有一個秘書的缺額。

17 dealing　[ˋdilɪŋ]　*n.*　行為；交易

Miranda is tough in her dealing with competitors.
米蘭達與競爭者交易時是強硬的。
financial dealings 商業往來

18 buyer　[ˋbaɪɚ]　*n.*　買主；買方

The buyer spent one million for the antique.
買家出價一百萬買那古董。
potential buyer 潛在的買家

主題 3

19 holder　[ˋholdɚ]　*n.*　持有人，所有人，支持物

It's illegal to reproduce photos without the permission of the copyright holder.
沒有經過版權所有人允許而複製相片是違法的。

20 revenue　[ˋrɛvəˏnju]　*n.*　收入；稅收

Interest is one form of revenue.
利息是一種收入。
advertising revenue 廣告收益
tax revenues 政府稅收

21 claim　[klem]　*n.*　要求；所有權；主張

The court denied claims that the man was murdered.
法庭否決那人是被謀殺的主張。

The woman asked a claim for compensation.

那女人要求賠償金。

false claims 錯誤的主張

22 **barely** 　['bɛrlɪ]　*adv.*　僅僅；勉強

The family have barely enough money to live on.

這家人僅有能維持家計的錢。

The shy student's voice is barely audible.

那害羞學生的聲音只能勉強聽的見。

barely visible 勉強看的見

23 **assent** 　[ə'sɛnt]　*vi.*　同意；贊成

My parents won't assent to my request to study from home.

我父母不會同意我離家讀書的請求。

The company has assented to the terms of our contract.

那公司已同意合約條款。

24 **forthwith** 　[forθ'wɪθ]　*adv.*　立刻；毫不猶豫地

Her child said good night and went back to her room forthwith.

她小孩道了晚安就立刻回房間。

They hope the training will cease forthwith.

他們希望訓練可以立刻停止。

【同】immediately, instantly

25 **trespass** 　['trɛspəs]　*n.　vi.*　擅自闖入；妨礙；冒犯

Jessie was arrested for trespassing on private property.

捷西因擅闖私人財產而被逮捕。

It's not allowed to trespass on railway property.

擅自闖入鐵路是不被允許的。

26 **downstairs** [ˌdaʊnˈstɛrz] *adv.* 往樓下 *adj.* 樓下的

He went downstairs in anger.

他生氣地走下樓。

My father was downstairs in the living room.

我父親在樓下的客廳。

27 **uneven** [ʌnˈivən] *adj.* 不平坦的；不公平的；不均等的

We toil on the muddy and uneven ground.

我們吃力走在泥濘不平坦的地面上。

an uneven distribution of resources 資源不平等分配

an uneven contest 不公平的競賽

28 **dungeon** [ˈdʌndʒən] *n.* 地牢

The prince was thrown into a dungeon under the castle.

那王子被關進城堡下的地牢。

29 **solid** [ˈsɑlɪd] *adj.* 固體的；牢固的 *n.* 固體

Ice is solid, water is liquid.

冰是固體，水是液體。

solid state 固體狀態

30 **workmanship** [ˈwɝkmənˌʃɪp] *n.* 手藝；工藝品

The watch is of matchless workmanship.

這支手錶作工精細。

主題 3

Unit 08

Mortgage 抵押借款

Track 32

1 beforehand [bɪˈforˌhænd] *adv.* 預先；提前地

Dinner had been arranged beforehand.

晚餐已提前安排好了。

2 rung [rʌŋ] *n.* 梯子的橫擋；椅腳的橫木

One of the rungs decayed.

其中的一層階梯蛀壞了。

on the highest/lowest rung of the ladder 在最高或最低階層

3 customary [ˈkʌstəmˌɛrɪ] *adj.* 慣常的；合乎習俗

It's customary to give children envelopes on Chinese New Year.

在農曆年給紅包是合乎習俗的。

4 lease [lis] *n.* 租；契約；租契

The landlord explained all the terms of the lease to the tenant.

房東向房課解釋租約裡的條款。

5 cheap [tʃip] *adj.* 廉價的；便宜的

Milk is very cheap now.

牛奶現在很便宜。

6 miser [`maɪzɚ] *n.* 守財奴；吝嗇鬼

Although Kevin is rich, he is an old miser.

雖然凱文很富有，但他是個老守財奴。

7 fulfill [fʊl`fɪl] *vt.* 履行；實踐

Visiting Europe has fulfilled my dream.

參觀歐洲已經實現了我的夢想。

fulfill an aim 實踐目標

fulfill oneself 完全實現自己的抱負

8 mortgage [`mɔrgɪdʒ] *n.* 抵押 *vt.* 抵押

He has paid off a 20-year mortgage.

他已付清二十年的貸款。

主題 3

9 banker [`bæŋkɚ] *n.* 銀行家

Vivian was a successful banker.

薇薇安是位成功的銀行家。

10 patron [`petrən] *n.* 贊助者；主顧

The patron donates 100 million dollars to the charity.

那贊助人捐款一百萬給慈善機構。

patron saint 守護神

11 vouchsafe [vaʊtʃ`sef] *vt.* 惠予；給予

He did not vouchsafe a reply.

他未予答覆。

12 assistance　[əˋsɪstəns]　*n.*　援助；幫助

The charity offers financial assistance to students.

這慈善機構提供財務協助給學生。

13 waver　[ˋwevɚ]　*vi.*　顫抖；搖擺；猶豫不決

While I was wavering, somebody else bought the dress.

我在猶豫不決時，別人就買了那件洋裝。

The student's attention began to waver as lunch time approached.

當午餐時間接近，那學生的專注力開始搖擺。

never waver from his loyalty 從未不忠

14 reckon　[ˋrɛkən]　*vi.*　計算　*vt.*　計算；認為

Did you reckon Dolly will accept my apology?

你認為朵莉會接受我的道歉嗎？

reckon sth. to be sth. 認為……應該是……

15 enormous　[ɪˋnɔrməs]　*adj.*　巨大的；龐大的

They spent an enormous amount of money to buy a mansion.

他們花了一大筆錢買一間豪宅。

16 apprehension　[͵æprɪˋhɛnʃən]　*n.*　恐懼；憂心

He arrived at office two hours early, filled with apprehension.

他很擔憂，提早二個小時到辦公室。

a feeling of apprehension 擔心的感覺

17 scare　　[skɛr]　*vt.*　驚嚇　*vi.*　受驚

The phone rang at midnight and scared me.

深夜的電話鈴聲嚇到我。

scare the pants off sb. 完全嚇到某人

18 sale　　[sel]　*n.*　賣；銷售

The local supermarket is holding a big sale.

當地的超市在舉行大拍賣。

19 adversity　　[əd`vɚsətɪ]　*n.*　不幸；逆境

The road to success is full of adversities.

通往成功之路充滿災難。

20 harry　　[`hærɪ]　*vt.*　騷擾；搶奪

The executive authorities have been harrying me for health insurance fee.

行政單位不斷要我繳交健保費用。

21 continuance　　[kən`tɪnjʊəns]　*n.*　繼續的期間，停留，持續

The continuance of war caused a lot of casualties.

戰事不斷帶來許多傷亡。

22 henceforth　　[ˌhɛs`forθ]　*adv.*　今後，從今以後

The guy said that he would work hard henceforth.

那男人說從今以後他要努力工作了。

Henceforth, I will be known as Mr. Woods.

從今以後我就是伍茲先生。

23 **millstone** [ˋmɪl͵ston] *n.* 石磨；重擔

The loan has been like a millstone round his neck.
那貸款像是壓在他身上的重擔。

a millstone round one's neck 某人身上的重擔

24 **guile** [gaɪl] *n.* 狡猾；奸詐

The fraud persuaded the woman to transfer accounts by guile.
那騙子狡猾地說服那女人轉帳。

The child might get what he wanted with a little guile.
那小孩利用一點奸詐來得到他想要的。

【同】cunning, deceit

25 **forfeit** [ˋfɔr͵fɪt] *vt.* 喪失　*n.* 喪失物

My mother forfeited her health due to years of hard work.
母親因多年艱苦工作而喪失健康。

John was ordered to forfeit his car for drunk driving.
約翰因酒駕而被沒收車子。

26 **dissolve** [dɪˋzɑlv] *vt.* *vi.* 溶解；解除（婚 等）；解散

We dissolved our engagement.
我們解除婚 。

My courage dissolved.
我沒有勇氣。

27 **lifetime** [ˋlaɪf͵taɪm] *n.* 一生；終身

He has encountered lots of hardship during his lifetime.

他一生中遭遇許多艱困。

My grandparents witnessed two world wars in the lifetime.

我祖父母在他們一生中見證二次世界大戰。

once in a lifetime 一生一次

28 slide [slaɪd] *vi.* 滑；滑落 *vt.* 使滑動；迅速地放置

Rice export slid by 30% this year.

今年的稻米出口量滑落百分之三十。

The boy slid the toy into his pocket while his mother was not looking.

當他媽媽沒看見時，男孩把玩具放進他的口袋。

Mandy slid down the bank into the river.

曼蒂從河岸滑進河裡。

29 abyss [əˋbɪs] *n.* 深淵；深坑

The country might plunge into an abyss of violence.

這國家可能陷入暴力的深淵。

Betty found her on the edge of an abyss.

貝蒂發現她的處境已在深淵邊緣。

30 privilege [ˋprɪvl̩ɪdʒ] *n.* 特權，優惠

It is a privilege to work with such organized people.

這是與這種有組織的人一起工作的一種特權。

The diplomat enjoys diplomatic privilege.

外交官享有外交特權。

主題 3

Architecture 建築學

Track 33

1 task　[tæsk]　*n.*　任務；工作；作業

It's an arduous task.

這是一項艱鉅的任務。

Her tasks were to wash and cook.

她的工作是洗衣和做飯。

a simple/difficult task 一個簡單／困難的任務

2 locate　[lo`ket]　*vt.*　把…設置在；座落於；找出

The headquarters is located in San Francisco.

總部座落於舊金山。

The police office is trying to locate the robber.

那員警設法找出搶匪。

3 locality　[lo`kælətɪ]　*n.*　地區；場所

There is a Chinese restaurant in this locality.

這地區有間中國餐館。

Here is a working-class locality.

這裡是勞工階級區。

4 situated　[`sɪtʃʊ,etɪd]　*adj.*　位於……的；處於……

There is a castle situated in the forest.

有座城堡位於森林中。

ideally located 理想地位於……

5　**architect**　[`ɑrkə,tɛkt]　*n.*　建築師；設計師

The architect created a structure for the new landmark building.

這建築師設計新地標建築的結構。

Each man is the architect of his or her own fate.

每個人都是他（她）自己命運的建築師。

6　**notable**　[`notəbl]　*adj.*　值得注意的；著名的

He was a notable lawyer.

他是一名著名的律師。

A notable feature of this temple is its carved pillars.

這寺廟著名的特色是雕刻的柱子。

notable achievement 顯要的成就

7　**figure**　[`fɪgjɚ]　*n.*　數字；外形；人物

The baseball player has become a figure known to everyone.

那棒球選手已成為知名人物。

8　**honorable**　[`ɑnərəbl]　*adj.*　值得尊敬的；光榮的；體面的

She is an honorable lady.

她是一個高尚的女士。

honorable mention 榮譽獎

honorable discharge 榮譽退役

9　**aristocratic**　[,ærɪstə`krætɪk]　*adj.*　貴族的；儀態高貴的

Richard comes from an aristocratic family.

理查出身貴族家庭。

aristocratic society 貴族社會

10 **ideal** [aɪˋdiəl] *adj.* 理想的；空想的

This path is an ideal place for a walk.

這小徑是散步的理想地點。

11 **contemporary** [kənˋtɛmpəˌrɛrɪ] *adj.* 當代的；同時代的 *n.* 同時代的人

She and I were contemporaries at college.

她和我是大學同期。

12 **precise** [prɪˋsaɪs] *adj.* 精確的；準確的

He caught the lady at the precise moment she fell down.

他在那女士跌倒時，在準確的一瞬間接住她。

13 **erect** [ɪˋrɛkt] *vt.* 建造；使豎立 *adj.* 直立的

The tower was erected last year.

這座塔是去年建造的。

Wilson stood erect on the stage.

威爾森在舞台上站得直直的。

14 **construct** [kənˋstrʌkt] *vt.* 建造；構成

The part was constructed to operate smoothly and without vibration.

這零件是為了運行平穩、無震動而建造的。

15 strengthen [`strɛŋθən] *vt.* 加 ；鞏固

The general has been brought in to strengthen the defense.
將軍被請來加強防禦。

16 adorn [ə`dɔrn] *vt.* 裝飾

Neon lights adorned the building's exterior.
霓虹燈裝飾著建築物外部。
The wall was adorned with paintings.
這道牆上裝飾許多畫。

17 oriental [,ori`ɛnt!] *adj.* 東方的 *n.* 東方人

The kid has oriental features.
這小孩有東方臉孔的特徵。

主題 3

18 ethereal [ɪ`θɪrɪəl] *adj.* 飄逸的；天上的

Lucia has an ethereal beauty.
露西亞美若天仙。
ethereal music 輕柔動聽的音樂

19 luminous [`lumənəs] *adj.* 發光的；照亮的；清楚的

A luminous glow shot from the sky.
一道亮光從天空射出。

20 harmonious [hɑr`monɪəs] *adj.* 和諧的；和睦的

The sky and the sea make a harmonious picture.
天空和大海構成一幅美麗的圖畫。

21 vertical [ˋvɝtɪk!] *adj.* 垂直的；豎的

Hank looked over the crag and found he was standing at the edge of a vertical drop.

漢克從峭壁俯視，發現他站在垂直落下的邊緣。

22 aerial [ˋɛrɪəl] *adj.* 空氣的；航空的

An aerial attack happened at midnight.

一場空襲在午夜發生。

23 forty [ˋfɔrtɪ] *n.* 四十；第四十

The emperor reigned over the empire for forty years.

這皇帝統治帝國四十年。

24 storey [ˋstorɪ] *n.* 樓層

Look at that eighteen-storey building!

看那棟十八層的大樓！

25 splendid [ˋsplɛndɪd] *adj.* 輝煌的；壯麗的

All the hotel rooms have splendid views.

飯店所有房間都有壯麗的風景。

A splendid church stood on the top of a steep hill.

一間壯麗的教堂轟立在陡丘的頂端。

win a splendid victory 贏得輝煌的勝利

26 incredible [ɪnˋkrɛdəb!] *adj.* 難以置信的

It's an incredible experience.

這是難以置信的經歷。

27 colossal   [kə`lɑsl]   *adj.*   巨大的

The celebration is a colossal waste of money.

這慶典是一大筆錢的浪費。

In the center of the city stood a colossal statue of the King.

在市中心矗立著一座國王的雕像。

28 gigantic   [dʒaɪ`gæntɪk]   *adj.*   巨大的；巨人似的

Hercules was a hero of gigantic strength in Greek mythology.

海克利斯是希臘神話中的大力士英雄。

The cost of building a skyscraper has been gigantic.

蓋一棟摩天樓的花費很龐大。

29 magnificence   [mæg`nɪfəsns]   *n.*   富麗堂皇；高尚莊嚴

The magnificence of the pyramids is admirable to every tourist.

金字塔的壯麗讓每位遊客都驚嘆不已。

Everyone was impressed with this magnificent performance.

每個人都對這場絕佳的表演印象深刻。

30 adventurous   [əd`vɛntʃərəs]   *adj.*   喜歡冒險的，大膽的，驚險的

The adventurous story is a fantasy.

冒險故事是一個虛構。

He is a daring and adventurous hiker.

他是位大膽和喜歡冒險的登山者。

主題 3

Neighborhood 鄰近地區

1 northwest [`nɔrθ`wɛst] *n.* 西北 *adj.* 位於西北的

The house is situated toward the northwest.

這房子的位置朝向西北。

The northwest of this country is the mountain area.

這國家的西北方是山區。

2 province [`pravɪns] *n.* 省；領域；範圍

Quebec is one of the provinces in Canada.

魁北克是加拿大的一省。

Chinese History is not my province.

中國歷史不是我的學術領域。

Marketing is the province of sales department.

行銷是業務部門的範圍。

3 seaport [`si,port] *n.* 海港；港口都市

Kaohsiung is a beautiful seaport.

高雄是個美麗的海港都市。

4 community [kə`mjunətɪ] *n.* 社區；社會；共同體

The post office will serve the whole community.

這間郵局將服務整個社區。

5 hamlet　[ˋhæmlɪt]　*n.*　村莊；部落；（大寫）Hamlet 哈姆雷特（莎士比亞悲劇）

Janet visited a hamlet in Italy last year.
珍娜去年參觀了一座在義大利的小村莊。

Hamlet is regarded as the classic example of a tragedy.
哈姆雷特被認為是經典的悲劇。

6 settlement　[ˋsɛt!mənt]　*n.*　解決；清算；殖民（地）

The two countries should look for a peaceful settlement to the dispute.
二國應尋求和平的解決爭端的方法。

out-of-court settlement 庭外和解

divorce settlement 離婚協議

peaceful settlement 和平落幕

主題 3

7 neighborhood　[ˋnebɚ͵hʊd]　*n.*　附近；鄰近地區

I grew up in a peaceful residential neighborhood.
我在一個平靜的住宅區長大。

8 immigrate　[ˋɪmə͵gret]　*vt.*　*vi.*　（使）遷徙；遷入

My grandparents immigrated to Australia after they retired.
我祖父母退休後移民到澳洲。

9 immigrant　[ˋɪməgrənt]　*n.*　移民　*adj.*　移民的；移入的

An illegal immigrant was caught by the police at the airport.
一名非法移民被警方在機場逮捕。

10 bring [brɪŋ] *vt.* 帶來；引出；促使

Power brings corruption.

權利帶來腐敗。

11 equal [`ikwəl] *adj.* 相等的；平等的

I believe all the subjects are of equal importance.

我相信所有的學科都一樣重要。

be equal to 等於

12 tranquility [træŋ`kwɪlətɪ] *n.* 寧靜

The elderly all like the tranquility of the country life.

年長者都喜歡鄉村生活的寧靜。

the tranquility of the countryside 鄉間的寧靜

13 tranquil [`træŋkwɪl] *adj.* 平靜的；穩定的

He stared at the tranquil surface of the sea.

他看著平靜的海面。

We live in a small tranquil village.

我們住在一個寧靜的小村莊。

14 adjacent [ə`dʒesənt] *adj.* 毗連的；連接的

I work in a company adjacent to a supermarket.

我在超市旁的一家公司工作。

15 lowly [`lolɪ] *adj.* 地位低的；卑微的；謙卑的

The successful CEO has a lowly heart.

這位成功的總裁有謙遜的心。

The monks lived in a lowly, humble residence.

這僧侶住在低下且簡陋的住所。

16 **agreeable**　　[əˋgriəb!]　　*adj.*　　宜人的；欣然同意的；一致的

Everyone in the meeting is agreeable to the proposal.

每位在會議中的人都同意這提議。

17 **parish**　　[ˋpærɪʃ]　　*n.*　　教區

The pious Christians go to the parish church every week.

虔誠的基督徒每周都去教區教堂。

parish pump 地方觀念的；目光狹隘的

18 **parson**　　[ˋpɑrsn]　　*n.*　　教區牧師

The parson of our church could be seen in the distance.

我們從很遠的地方就可以看見教堂尖塔。

19 **chapel**　　[ˋtʃæp!]　　*n.*　　小禮拜堂；禮拜儀式

The chapel was dedicated in 1850.

這座小教堂於 1850 年舉行獻堂裡。

wedding chapel 結婚禮堂

20 **cathedral**　　[kəˋθidrəl]　　*n.*　　大教堂

A cathedral is a religious building for worship.

大教堂是一個供人做禮拜的宗教建築物。

This cathedral is designed by a famous architect.

這座大教堂是由一位有名的建築師所設計。

主題 **3**

21 spire   [spaɪr]   *n.*   （教堂）尖頂；尖塔

The spire of the church could be seen in the distance.

我們從很遠的地方就可以看見教堂尖塔。

22 stout   [staʊt]   *adj.*   矮胖的；牢固的；不屈饒的；猛烈的

She's growing rather stout.

她有點發胖。

23 shrine   [ʃraɪn]   *n.*   聖壇；神龕；聖地

Every weekend the old man went to worship at the shrine.

這老先生每個周末會去神壇拜拜。

The Louvre is a shrine to the French artists.

羅浮宮是法國藝術家的聖地。

a pilgrimage to the shrine of 去……的聖殿朝聖

24 migrate   [ˈmaɪˌgret]   *vi.*   遷徙；移居

Asians begin to migrate to the United States in the early 20th century.

亞洲人在二十世紀初期開始移民美國。

25 stray   [stre]   *vi.*   迷路；偏離   *adj.*   迷路的

I was attacked by a stray dog.

我被流浪狗攻擊。

The discussion is starting to stray from the point.

討論一開始就偏離主題。

a stray dog 流浪狗

26 transfer　[træns`fɝ]　*vt.*　轉換；改變　*vi.*　轉移；換車

The aging chairman is going to transfer power to his son.

年邁的董事者將把權力轉給兒子。

Passengers to Taipei need to transfer at this station.

要到台北的旅客須在本站換車。

27 encounter　[ɪn`kaʊntɚ]　*vt.*　遭遇；遇到（困難）；偶遇

n.　遭遇

Sarah encountered difficulties after she lost her arm in a car accident.

在車禍喪失一隻手後，莎拉面臨困境。

a fortunate encounter 邂逅

28 boyhood　[`bɔɪhʊd]　*n.*　少年時代

My boyhood memories come alive.

我童年回憶歷歷在目。

【反】girlhood

29 gang　[gæŋ]　*n.*　一幫；一夥

There is a gang of kids hanging around on the street.

有一群年輕人總是在街上閒晃。

30 acquaintance　[ə`kwentəns]　*n.*　相識；了解；熟人

The couple developed an acquaintance over the Internet.

這對情侶是在網路上認識的。

have a nodding acquaintance of sth. 對……有粗略的了解

主題 3

Agent 代理商

Track 35

1 mister [ˋmɪstɚ] *n.* 先生（通常縮寫為 Mr.）

Thanks for your help, mister.

謝謝你的幫忙，先生。

2 salesman [ˋselzmən] *n.* 推銷員

An aggressive salesman will achieve remarkable success.

一位積極的推銷員會達到顯著的成績。

3 suspicious [səˋspɪʃəs] *adj.* 可疑的；猜

His vibrating voice made us suspicious.

他顫抖的聲音令我懷疑。

in suspicious circumstances 可疑情況下

4 hasty [ˋhestɪ] *adj.* 匆忙的；倉促輕率的

My sister has a hasty breakfast and then rushed to the train station.

我姊姊匆忙吃了早餐就衝往火車站。

a hasty conclusion 一個輕率的結論

5 fraud [frɔd] *n.* 欺騙；騙子

I feel like a fraud when lying to my wife.

當我向太太撒謊時，我感覺我像是個騙子。

insurance fraud 保險詐欺

6 sly [slaɪ] *adj.* 狡猾的；悄悄的

Don't believe his words; he is a sly old fox.

相信他；他像老狐狸一樣狡猾。

【同】wily, cunning

7 deceit [dɪˋsit] *n.* 欺騙；欺詐

The film is about theft and deceit on the social scale.

這電影是有關社會階級的偷竊與詐欺。

calculated deceit 計畫好的騙局

8 credulity [krɪˋdjulətɪ] *n.* 輕信；易受騙

The playboy has practiced on my credulity.

這花花公子利用了我的信任。

strain credulity 很難相信

9 dispute [dɪˋspjut] *vi.* *vt.* *n.* 爭論；爭執

The minister was involved in a political dispute.

那位部長陷入一場政治爭論中。

settle a dispute 解決爭執

domestic dispute 家庭爭論

10 separation [ˌsɛpəˋreʃən] *n.* 分離；分開；分居

Most people suffer the separation of family during wartime.

大部分的人在戰時都遭受家庭分崩離析。

separation anxiety（嬰兒）分離焦慮

trial separation 分開偵訊

racial separation 種族分離

11 **recommend** [ˌrɛkəˈmɛnd] *vt.* 推薦；介紹；勸告

I recommend that you get a health examination.

我勸你去做健康檢查。

Mandy strongly recommended this book to everyone with an interest in history.

曼蒂強力推薦這本書給每個對歷史有興趣的人。

12 **sincere** [sɪnˈsɪr] *adj.* 真誠的；正直的

I make my sincere apologies to Jenny.

我向珍妮獻上誠摯的歉意。

sincere gratitude 真摯的感謝

13 **sincerity** [sɪnˈsɛrətɪ] *n.* 真誠；誠意

Misfortune tests the sincerity of friends.

【諺】患難見真情。

The man delivered a speech with deep sincerity.

這人用深深的誠摯發表了一場演講。

the sincerity of his belief 他信仰的誠心誠意

14 **entirely** [ɪnˈtaɪrlɪ] *adv.* 完全地；徹底地

Her success is entirely due to a diligent attitude.

她的成功完全歸因於勤勉的態度。

The earthquake entirely destroyed the town.

地震完全摧毀了這城鎮。

15 decent [ˋdisn̩t] *adj.* 正派的；體面的；親切的

Maria wore a decent dress to attend the graduation ceremony.

瑪莉亞穿了一件合乎禮儀的洋裝參加畢業典禮。

It is very decent of you to help.

你真是樂於助人。

16 capable [ˋkepəbl̩] *adj.* 有能力的；有才能的

Julia is capable of dealing with complicated situations.

茱莉亞很有能力處理複雜情況。

capable hands 有將事情處理好的能力

17 agency [ˋedʒənsɪ] *n.* 代辦處；經銷商；仲介；局

Frank went to the travel agency to get some information about the trip to Tibet.

法蘭克到旅行社要些有關到西藏旅行的資訊。

18 passionate [ˋpæʃənɪt] *adj.* 熱情的；熱烈的；易怒的

Debbie gave her boyfriend a passionate kiss.

黛比給了男友一記熱情的吻。

make a passionate speech 做一場熱情洋溢的演講

19 trusty [ˋtrʌstɪ] *adj.* 可信任的；可信賴的；可靠的

My trusty flashlight will light us the way in the dark woods.

我這可靠的手電筒會在黑暗的樹林裡為我們照亮路。

Jason ran the marathon with his trusty jogging shoes.

主題 3

傑森穿著他信賴的慢跑鞋跑這場馬拉松。

20 **prompt** [prɑmpt] *adj.* 敏捷的；及時的　*vt.* 促使；引起

The bank clerk made a prompt reply to my inquiry.

銀行行員對我的詢問做了一個及時的答覆。

prompt action 及時行動

21 **consultation** [ˌkɑnsəl`teʃən] *n.* 諮詢；商議；診察

Terry chose his major in consultation with his teacher.

泰瑞和他的老師諮詢他的主修科目。

22 **espouse** [ɪs`paʊz] *vi.* 支持；擁護

This party espouses the democratic philosophy.

這政黨支持民主哲學。

espouse a policy 支持政策

23 **fundamental** [ˌfʌndə`mɛntl̩] *adj.* 基礎的；基本的

Everyone was born with fundamental rights.

每個人與生俱來基本的人權。

24 **bargain** [`bɑrgɪn] *n.* 交易　*vi.* 議價；達成協議

There is a bargain in the jewelry store.

珠寶店內政有一筆交易。

make a bargain with sb. 和某人做了一項交易

25 **lightly** [`laɪtlɪ] *adv.* 輕輕的；少量的；輕率地

The father walked lightly in order not to wake his son.

這父親輕輕地走路以免吵醒兒子。

Marriage is a matter you can't afford to take lightly.

婚姻是一件你不能輕率對待的事。

26 **indirect** [ˌɪndəˈrɛkt] *adj.* 間接的;不坦率的

An indirect result of smoking is losing weight.

抽菸的間接結果就是會體重減輕。

27 **sway** [swe] *vi.* *vt.* 搖擺;傾斜

The trees are swaying gently in the breeze.

樹在微風中輕擺。

The wave caused the fishing rod to sway from side to side.

波浪使釣魚竿左右擺動。

28 **actual** [ˈæktʃʊəl] *adj.* 實際的;事實上的

I am not kidding. Those are her actual words.

我不是開玩笑。她真的這樣說。

29 **administer** [ədˈmɪnəstə] *vt.* 管理;執行

The courts administer justice.

法院執行正義。

30 **enquiring** [ɪnˈkwaɪrɪŋ] *adj.* 好問的;愛打聽的;探詢的

My brother has an enquiring mind.

我弟弟有探究精神。

Insurance 保險

Track 36

1　statute　[ˋstætʃʊt]　*n.*　法令；條例

Protection for employees was laid down by statute.

法律建立了對員工的保護。

statue book 法令全書

statute law 成文法

2　merit　[ˋmɛrɪt]　*n.*　價值；長處；功績

The cartoon has the merit of being educational.

這卡通有具教育性的特點。

The film is full of artistic merits.

這電影充滿藝術價值。

literary merit 文學價值

3　invariable　[ɪnˋvɛrɪəbl!]　*adj.*　不變的；恆定的

My route to school is invariable.

我上學的路線是不變的。

4　insure　[ɪnˋʃʊr]　*vt.*　為⋯投保

I want to insure my car.

我要為車保險。

insure yourself against sth. 保護自己遠離⋯⋯

5 **advocate** [ˋædvəkɪt] *n.* 提倡者 *vt.* 擁護；提倡

Janet is a passionate advocate of vegetarianism.

珍娜是個素食主義的激昂提倡者。

This organization advocates natural childbirth.

這團體提倡自然生產。

6 **protector** [prəˋtɛktɚ] *n.* 保護者；防禦者

Parents are protectors of their babies.

父母是孩子的保護者。

Miranda is an enthusiastic protector of individual liberties.

米蘭達是個人自由權的狂熱保護者。

7 **league** [lig] *n.* 聯盟

Several Asia countries formed a defense league.

幾個亞洲國家組成防禦聯盟。

主題 **3**

8 **association** [ə͵sosɪˋeʃən] *n.* 協會；社團；結合

Mr. Chen has joined the teachers' association for three years.

陳老師已加入教師公會三年。

in association with sth./sb. 與……的聯合

9 **classification** [͵klæsəfəˋkeʃən] *n.* 分類；分級；分類法

Hank is responsible for the classification of fruits according to the quality.

漢克是負責根據品質做水果分級。

job classification 工作分類

10 **arrangement** [əˋrendʒmənt] *n.* 整理;安排

Gina volunteered to help with arrangements for the party.

吉娜自願幫忙派對安排。

security arrangements 安檢布置

11 **contemplate** [ˋkɑntɛmˏplet] *vt. vi.* 思量

Tracy is contemplating resigning.

翠西正考慮要辭職。

12 **ascertain** [ˏæsɚˋten] *vt.* 查明確定;弄清

I ascertained that he was murdered.

我確定他是被謀殺的。

13 **maze** [mez] *n.* 迷;困惑

The boy was lost in the maze for two hours.

男孩在迷宮裡迷路了二個小時。

maze of tunnels 迂迴的隧道

maze of regulations(複雜)規定的困惑

in a maze 困惑

14 **arithmetic** [əˋrɪθmətɪk] *n.* 算術;計算 *adj.* 算術的

I'm good at science but not so hot at arithmetic.

我對科學在行;但算術不好。

mental arithmetic 心算

arithmetic mean 算術平均

arithmetic progression 等差級數

15 quote　[kwot]　*vt.*　*vi.*　引用；引證　*vt.*　報價

He quotes from the magazine article.

他從一篇雜誌文章引證。

The designer has quoted one million to cut out a garment.

設計師對裁剪衣服報價一百萬。

quote a passage from… 從……引用一段文字

16 approval　[ə`pruv!]　*n.*　贊成；同意；批准

The research has received official approval.

此研究已取得官方許可。

17 renew　[rɪ`nju]　*vt.*　使更新　*vi.*　更新

I need to renew my driving license this year.

我今年需要更新駕照。

18 policy　[`pɑləsɪ]　*n.*　政策；方針

The government policy on economy will be reformed next year.

政府的經濟政策明年會進行改革。

insurance policy 保單

19 mishap　[`mɪs,hæp]　*n.*　不幸事故；災難

Phone your family that you have arrived here without mishap.

打電話告訴給家人你已平安抵達。

without mishap 平安無事

20 storm [stɔrm] *n.* 暴風雨

There is a storm coming from the Pacific.

有個風暴正從太平洋過來。

storm petrel 引起爭端的人

21 havoc [`hævək] *n.* 大破壞；浩劫

The tsunami has made great havoc of the island.

海嘯給這島嶼帶來巨大的破壞。

22 evidence [`ɛvədəns] *n.* 證據；證詞；證人

We still haven't found any evidence of life on other planets.

我們仍然沒有發現其他星球有生命的證據。

23 unreasonable [ʌn`riznəb!] *adj.* 不講道理的；不合理的

It's unreasonable to ask your employees to work twelve hours a day.

要求你的員工一天工作十二小時是不合理的。

24 unsettled [ʌn`sɛt!d] *adj.* 不穩定的；未解決的

The dispute remains unsettled.

爭端尚未解決。

The weather is unsettled, you should not drive out.

天氣還不穩定，你應該不要開車出門。

25 notify [`notə,faɪ] *vt.* 通知；告知；報告

Please notify us of any change of phone number.

電話號碼若有更換，請通知我們。

26 heir　[ɛr]　*n.*　繼承人；嗣子

Prince Jonathan is the heir to the throne.

強納森王子是王為繼承人。

heir apparent 法定繼承人

27 succession　[sək`sɛʃən]　*n.*　連續；繼承（權）

He ran the marathon five times in succession.

他連續參加五次馬拉松。

Divorce will prevent the prince's succession to the throne.

離婚會使王子喪失王位繼承權。

28 pertain　[pɚ`ten]　*vi.*　附屬；關於；相配

We only care about the issue that pertains to the industrial pollution.

我們只在意工業污染的議題。

主題 3

29 covenant　[`kʌvɪnənt]　*n.*　契約　*vi.*　*vt.*　立約承諾

The billionaire covenanted to pay two million dollars a year to help the orphans.

億萬富翁立約承諾每年付二百萬幫助孤兒。

The agreement contained a covenant against nuclear weapons.

這協定裡包含反核武的契約。

30 acknowledge　[ək`nɑlɪdʒ]　*vt.*　承認；告知收到

She is acknowledged as one of the top experts in the field.

她被公認為是該領域的頂尖專家之一。

主題 4

Technology & Science

科技與科學

Computer 電腦

Track 37

1 precede   [prɪˋsid]   *vt.*   在……之前   *vi.*   領先

He let the lady precede him through the door.

他先讓女士通過門。

Dessert will be preceded by the speech from the manager.

甜點在經理的演講前會先送上來。

precede sth. with 以……為序幕

2 conception   [kənˋsɛpʃən]   *n.*   概念，觀念，想法

I have a conception of people as being basically good.

我認為人性本善。

have no conception of 不知道

3 imaginary   [ɪˋmædʒəˏnɛrɪ]   *adj.*   想像中的，假想的

Children still have a general fear for imaginary infernal powers.

孩童們對於虛構的地獄鬼神仍具有一種普遍的恐懼。

4 wonderful   [ˋwʌndəfəl]   *adj.*   極好的，精彩的

The Great Wall is a wonderful sight.

長城的景色令人歎為觀止。

a wonderful story 一個奇妙的故事

5 substantial [səb`stænʃəl] *adj.* 物質的；堅固的；大量的

The building is substantial enough to last a century.

這房子很堅固，一世紀也不會壞。

We have the support of a substantial number of teachers.

我們獲得許多老師的支持。

a substantial dinner 一頓豐盛的晚餐

6 nimble [`nɪmb!] *adj.* 敏捷的，靈活的

Grandma knitted a scarf for me with her nimble fingers.

祖母用靈巧的雙手為我織了一條圍巾。

a nimble mind / brain 聰明的頭腦

7 apparatus [ˌæpə`retəs] *n.* 器械，儀器；器官；機構

There are some electrical apparatus in the factory.

工廠裡有些電器。

The apparatus of government has become corrupt.

政府機關已經腐敗。

breathing apparatus 呼吸器官

8 speedy [`spidɪ] *adj.* 快的，迅速的

The patient had a speedy revival after his heart surgery.

那個病人在心臟手術後迅速康復。

a speedy recovery from injury 從傷害中快速復原

9 electrical [ɪ`lɛktrɪk!] *adj.* 電的，電氣科學的

The electrical system is out of control.

電路系統失控。

主題 4

electrical storm 夾帶閃電的暴風

10 **artificial**　[ˌɑrtəˋfɪʃəl]　*adj.*　人工的；矯揉造作的

Artificial fertilizer hastens the growth of plants.
人工肥料能促進植物生長。
artificial surgery 整形
artificial intelligence 人工智慧

11 **equip**　[ɪˋkwɪp]　*vt.*　裝備，配備

My office is well equipped.
我的辦公室裝備良好。

12 **successive**　[səkˋsɛsɪv]　*adj.*　連續的；接連的

The baseball team has had three successive victories.
這棒球隊已連贏三場比賽。

13 **shipment**　[ˋʃɪpmənt]　*n.*　裝貨；裝載的貨物

The freighter with the oil shipment anchored in the harbor.
載油的貨輪停在港口。

14 **ware**　[wɛr]　*n.*　商品，貨物；物品

He sells his wares at the big computer market.
他在大型電腦市場銷售自己的商品。

15 **hardware**　[ˋhɑrd͵wɛr]　*n.*　五金器具；硬體

We need to buy extra education hardware.
我們需要再買額外的教學設備。

I need to buy something from the hardware shop.

我需要去五金行買東西。

16 **metal** [ˋmɛt!] *n.* 金屬

A small silver metal box clattered down the stone stairs.

一個銀色金屬盒子沿著石階滾了下去，發出噹啷聲。

17 **knob** [nɑb] *n.* 門把，拉手；旋鈕

When her husband turned the knob, the noise diminished.

她丈夫一轉旋鈕，雜音就變小了。

18 **hack** [hæk] *vi.* *vt.* 亂劈，亂砍

The farmer was hacking at a tree.

農夫正在砍樹。

hack sth. off / down 砍斷……

19 **hijack** [ˈhaɪdʒæk] *vt.* 搶劫，劫持，揩油

The terrorists planned to hijack a plane.

恐怖份子們計畫劫持一架飛機。

The school bus was hijacked by a criminal.

校車被一個罪犯劫持。

主題 4

20 **random** [ˋrændəm] *n.* 隨機 *adj.* 隨機的

Magazines were piled up on the shelf at random.

雜誌胡亂地堆放在架上。

choose at random 隨機挑選

21 **troublesome**　[ˋtrʌbḷsəm]　*adj.*　令人煩惱的

The meeting has proven more troublesome than we expected.

會議遠超過我們預期的棘手。

troublesome itching 癢得難受

22 **bug**　[bʌg]　*n.*　臭蟲；（美）蟲子，故障

I find some bugs in the program.

我發現電腦程式有些問題。

catch / pick up a bug 小傳染病

23 **defect**　[dɪˋfɛkt]　*n.*　缺點，缺陷，欠缺

The new cell phone had to be withdrawn from the market because of a mechanical defect.

那種新手機因有機械缺陷只好撤出市場。

a genetic defect 基因缺陷

24 **baffle**　[ˋbæfḷ]　*vt.*　使挫折　*n.*　迷惑

The beautiful sunset baffles description.

這美麗的日落難以形容。

The math question baffled Tom completely.

湯姆被這數學問題打敗。

25 **insert**　[ɪnˋsɝt]　*vt.*　插入；嵌入；登載

The doorman inserted the key in the lock.

門房人員把鑰匙插入鎖中。

My teacher inserts her comment in the space of this page.

老師把評語插入這頁的空白處。

26 scan [skæn] *vt.* *n.*　細看；流覽；掃描

The little girl scanned the street for her mother.

小女孩掃視街道找媽媽。

brain scan 腦部掃描

27 undo [ʌn`du] *vt.*　解開，打開；取消

The girl undid the package.

這女孩打開了行李。

28 quicken [`kwɪkən] *vt.* *vi.*　加快

Sarah felt her heart quicken when she caught sight of Robert.

當莎拉看見羅勃時，她覺得心跳加快。

29 amusement [ə`mjuzmənt] *n.*　娛樂，消遣，樂趣

Julian finds amusement in collecting coins.

茱莉安發現了收集硬幣的樂趣。

主題 4

30 enjoyment [ɪn`dʒɔɪmənt] *n.*　享樂；欣賞

Singing has brought me great enjoyment.

唱歌帶給我極大的享受。

Mobile 手機

Track 38

1　inspiration　[ˌɪnspəˋreʃən]　*n.*　鼓舞；激動人心的人；靈感

My friend was a constant inspiration to me.

我的朋友是不斷鼓舞我前進的人。

provoke inspiration 激起靈感

2　herald　[ˋhɛrəld]　*n.*　傳令官；預示　*vt.*　通報；預示……來臨

A herald announces the message.

傳令官宣布訊息。

A flash of lightning heralded the heavy rain.

閃電即是下大雨的徵兆。

herald of sth. 預告……的來臨

3　introduction　[ˌɪntrəˋdʌkʃən]　*n.*　介紹；引進；引言

I'm reading an introduction of a series of the books.

我正在閱讀這一系列書籍的簡介。

4　virtue　[ˋvɝtʃu]　*n.*　善，德；德行；優點

Mother Teresa is a paragon of virtue.

德雷莎修女是美德的典範。

Among his many virtues are honesty, justice, and courage.

誠實、正義與勇氣都是他的優點。

5 movable [`muvəb!] *n.* 傢俱，動產 *adj.* 可移動的

The man's movables are worth a lot.

這人的動產價值不菲。

Henry bought his son a robot with movable arms and legs.

亨利買給兒子一個手腳會移動的機器人。

6 convenience [kən`vinjəns] *n.* 便利，方便；廁所

We find our folding chair a great convenience.

我們發現可折疊的椅子使用非常方便。

7 astonishing [ə`stɑnɪʃɪŋ] *adj.* 令人驚訝的

How astonishing!

真驚人！

an astonishing decision 驚人的決定

8 fantastic [fæn`tæstɪk] *adj.* 空想的；奇異的

We watched a fantastic performance in the National Theatre.

我們在國家劇院看了一場非常精彩的演出。

a fantastic scheme 不現實的計畫

主題 4

9 supreme [sə`prim] *adj.* 最高的；最大的

The captain was given supreme power.

船長被授予最高權力。

make the supreme sacrifice 為（國）作最大犧牲

10 **ingenious**　[ɪnˋdʒinjəs]　*adj.*　機靈的；精巧製成的

This research shows that Chris is an ingenious professor.
這個研究顯示克里斯是一個足智多謀的教授。

Many birds have ingenious ways to protect their nestlings.
許多鳥有機靈的方式保護雛鳥。

11 **compact**　[kəmˋpækt]　*adj.*　緊密的；小巧的　*vt.*　使緊湊

Women like the compact design of toys.
女人喜歡玩物小巧的設計。

The grass grew in a compact mass.
草長得滿地一片。

12 **tiny**　[ˋtaɪnɪ]　*adj.*　微小的，極小的

Ants are tiny insects.
螞蟻是很小的昆蟲。

The old man lived in a tiny house all by himself.
老人獨自一人地住在小房子裡。

tiny minority 極少數

13 **battery**　[ˋbætərɪ]　*n.*　電池，炮兵連；兵器群

A captain commands a company or battery.
一個上尉指揮一個連隊或炮兵連。

change the batteries in sth. 換……的電池

charge a battery 充電

14 **charger**　[ˋtʃɑrdʒɚ]　*n.*　充電器，襲擊者，軍馬

Please put my charger into your bag.

請把我的充電器放到你的袋裡。

15 jack [dʒæk] *n.* 起重器；傳動裝置 *vt.* 用舉重機、千斤頂舉起

They've jacked up the price.

他們已經把價格抬高了。

Ryan jacked the car to change the tire.

萊恩頂起車子以更換輪胎。

jack in my job 辭職

16 durable [`djʊrəb!] *adj.* 耐久的，耐用的

The closet is very durable.

衣櫃很耐用。

17 fixture [`fɪkstʃə] *n.* 固定裝置，配件；固定某工作或活動的人

The price doesn't include all fixtures and fittings.

這個價錢不包括所有的固定裝置和設備。

主題 4

18 casual [`kæʒʊəl] *adj.* 偶然的；隨便的

Jessica tried to appear casual at this party.

潔西卡試圖在這派對上顯得隨便一點。

Janet gave me a casual glance as she walked by.

珍娜經過我時，瞥過我一眼。

19 call [kɔl] *vt.* 把 ... 叫做；叫，喊

I will go and call him.

我去叫他。

20 **converse** [kənˋvɝs] *vi.* 交談

I conversed with my friend for hours on the phone.
我和朋友在電話裡談了幾小時。

Roy enjoyed the chance to converse with another English speaker.
羅伊很開心有機會與另一個說英語者交談。

21 **interrupt** [ˌɪntəˋrʌpt] *vt.* 打斷（講話）；打擾

Sorry to interrupt, but I need your help now.
抱歉打擾，但我現在需要你幫忙。

22 **fuss** [fʌs] *n.* 忙亂；吹捧 *vi.* 忙亂

Jason always makes a fuss over such a trifle.
傑森總是為這種小事大驚小怪。

I'd better go back home or there'd be a fuss.
我最好快回家，不然事情會一團糟。

23 **alarm** [əˋlɑrm] *n.* 驚恐；警報 *vt.* 使驚慌恐懼

The official is alarmed by the dramatic increase in murders.
官方對謀殺案件的急劇增加感到憂慮。

in alarm 保持警覺

24 **wail** [wel] *vi.* *vt.* *n.* 哀號，痛哭

A child couldn't find her mother and began to wail.
小孩找不到媽媽而嚎啕大哭。

25 **emergency**   [ɪ`mɝdʒənsɪ]   *n.*   緊急情況，突然事件

Nurses are trained to deal with emergencies.

護士受過處理緊急狀況的訓練。

emergency room 加護病房

26 **SOS**   [`ɛs,o`ɛs]   *n.*   緊急求救信號

The ship is sinking, and I have to send an SOS.

船要沉了，我不得不發出緊急求救信號。

SOS 為 save our soul 的縮寫。

27 **impatient**   [ɪm`peʃənt]   *adj.*   不耐煩的，急躁的

William turned around with an impatient expression.

威廉一臉不耐煩地轉過頭來。

28 **resound**   [rɪ`zaʊnd]   *vi.*   迴響，鳴響，傳遍，馳名

The circus tent resounded with cheers.

馬戲團中充滿喝采聲。

主題 4

29 **distinct**   [dɪ`stɪŋkt]   *adj.*   獨特的；清楚的

Those two languages are quite distinct from each other.

這兩種語言截然不同。

30 **prevail**   [prɪ`vel]   *vi.*   勝，優勝；流行

This tradition prevails over the whole country.

這一傳統在整個國家盛行。

Samantha's merits will enable her to prevail over difficulties.

莎曼莎的優點能讓她戰勝困難。

Unit 03　Multimedia 多媒體

Track 39

1　newly　[ˋnjulɪ]　*adv.*　新近，最近

The newly appointed director was a professor.

新任命的處長是位教授。

2　foremost　[ˋfor͵most]　*adj.*　最初的；第一流的

Chopin was considered the world's foremost composer.

蕭邦被認為是世界一流的作曲家。

foremost authority on ⋯⋯方面的權威

3　edition　[ɪˋdɪʃən]　*n.*　版，版本，版次

This US edition of the fiction is sold out.

美國版本的雜誌已售完了。

4　successful　[səkˋsɛsfəl]　*adj.*　成功的，結果良好的

The scholar later became successful in politics.

這名學者後來在政治方面很成功。

5　magic　[ˋmædʒɪk]　*n.*　魔法，巫術；戲法

The wonderful scenery began to work its magic and I started to relax.

美麗的風景產生魔法，我開始放鬆。

6 digital [ˋdɪdʒɪtl̩] *adj.* 數位的，計數的

It's the first digital magazine in China.

它是中國第一本數位雜誌。

7 entertainment [͵ɛntɚˋtenmənt] *n.* 招待，招待會；娛樂

This regulation applies to all places of public entertainment.

這一規定適用於一切公共娛樂場所。

the entertainment business / industry 娛樂業

8 gorgeous [ˋgɔrdʒəs] *adj.* 絢麗的；極好的

As the sun goes down, the rosy clouds are gorgeous.

日落時分的雲霞絢麗多彩。

9 spectacle [ˋgɔrdʒəs] *n.* 光景，景象；眼鏡

It's a strange spectacle to see these two enemies shaking hands.

這二個仇家握手真是個奇怪的景象。

make a spectacle of yourself 讓自己陷入窘境

10 amaze [əˋmez] *vt.* 使驚奇，使驚愕

Mona amazed her friends by suddenly getting divorced.

夢娜突然離婚讓朋友訝異。

11 amazement [əˋmezmənt] *n.* 驚異，詫異

She stared at him in amazement.

她驚異地瞪著他看。

主題 4

¹² rouse　[raʊz]　*vt.*　喚醒，喚起；驚起

The explosion roused the residents nearby.

爆炸讓附近居民驚醒。

rouse sb. from sleep / dreams 把⋯⋯從睡夢中喚醒

¹³ objection　[əb`dʒɛkʃən]　*n.*　反對，異議；不喜歡

You've no objection, I trust.

我相信你不反對吧。

strong objection 強烈反對

raise an objection to sth. 反對⋯⋯

do sth. over the objections of sb. 不顧某人反對做⋯⋯

¹⁴ bass　[`bes]　*n.*　低音樂器；男低音

Willy has a fine bass voice.

威利的聲音低沉悅耳。

¹⁵ sound　[saʊnd]　*adj.*　健康的；完好的　*n.*　聲音

We arrived home safe and sound.

我們平安到家。

¹⁶ grate　[gret]　*vt.*　磨碎　*vi.*　使人煩躁

That loud music grates on my ears.

那震耳欲聾的音樂使我耳朵受不了。

Peel and grate the carrots.

把紅蘿蔔削皮後磨碎。

grate on 惹惱

17 **overwhelm** [ˌovəˈhwɛlm] *vt.* 壓倒，使不知所措

If I cannot overwhelm with my creation, I will overwhelm
with my quality.

如果我不能以創意壓倒群雄，我就一定要以質感取勝。

Grief overwhelmed me.

悲傷襲擊我。

18 **hoarse** [hors] *adj.* 發音嘶啞的

Allen's voice sounded hoarse.

艾倫說話聲音嘶啞。

19 **faint** [fent] *adj.* 暗淡的；微弱的

I heard a faint sound of a train in the distance.

我聽到遠處有個微弱的火車聲音。

The faint light of dawn slanted from the window.

微弱的曙光從窗戶斜射進來。

20 **lag** [læg] *vi.* 走得慢 *n.* 落後

Some of the players in the game began to lag.

參加比賽的球員中有一些開始落後了。

Several children are tired and lagged behind their teacher.

幾個小孩累了跟著走在老師後面。

21 **exaggerate** [ɪgˈzædʒəˌret] *vt.* *vi.* 誇大，誇張

I couldn't eat for two days-I am not exaggerating.

我不誇張，我已經二天無法進食。

22 magnify　['mægnə,faɪ]　*vt.*　放大，擴大

Telescopes and microscopes magnify.
望遠鏡和顯微鏡能放大物體。

23 restrain　[rɪ'stren]　*vt.*　抑制，制止，遏制

The naughty boy couldn't restrain his curiosity.
頑皮的男孩抑制不住自己的好奇心。
restrain oneself 自我克制

24 consequently　['kɑnsə,kwɛntlɪ]　*adv.*　因此，因而，所以

I spent most of my energy in the first round and consequently lost the contest.
我在第一回合花掉大部分的力氣，因此輸了比賽。

25 extra　['ɛkstrə]　*adj.*　額外的　*adv.*　特別地

Christine is so envious of me getting an extra bonus.
克莉絲汀很羨慕我得到額外的獎金。
have a lot of extra work 有許多額外的工作

26 personal　['pɝsn̩]　*adj.*　個人的；本人的

I know from personal experience that Larry is unreliable.
從我個人經驗中知道賴瑞是靠不住的。
I must insist upon my personal opinion.
我必須堅持我個人的見解。
personal quality 個人特質

27 **vivid**   [ˋvɪvɪd]   *adj.*   鮮豔的；生動的

Those vivid memories came to his mind suddenly.
那些鮮明的回憶突然湧上他的心頭。
vivid imagination 生動的想像

28 **resolution**   [͵rɛzəˋluʃən]   *n.*   堅決，堅定；決定

Unfortunately, Bryan cannot shake her resolution.
不幸的是，布萊恩無法動搖她的決心。
The workers had failed to agree to the resolution.
工人們無法同意這決定。
pass a resolution 通過決定

29 **comparison**   [kəmˋpærəsn]   *n.*   比較，對照；比擬

Luke is rather smart in comparison with others.
和別人比較起來，路克相當聰明。
The analysis was provided for comparison with the result of previous research.
這分析是用來與之前的研究作比較。

30 **consider**   [kənˋsɪdɚ]   *vt.*   考慮；把……看作

In judging Susan, you should consider her age.
在對蘇珊進行評審時，你應該考慮到她的年紀。

Internet 網路

Track 40

1 web [wεb] *n.* 網，絲，網狀物

The web page is designed by a junior high school student.
這網頁是一名國中生設計的。

a tangled web of relations 錯綜複雜的關係

2 prominent [ˋprɑmənənt] *adj.* 實起的；突出的；顯著的

Cathleen has a lean, gaunt frame with prominent bones.
凱薩琳的身材骨瘦如柴。

Erwin was a prominent German scientist.
愛爾文是德國一位重要的科學家。

play a prominent part 扮演重要的角色

3 invisible [ɪnˋvɪzəb!] *adj.* 看不見的，無形的

These bacteria are invisible to the naked eye.
這些細菌用肉眼看不見。

The fighter is meant to be invisible from radar.
這戰鬥機無法從雷達被偵測到。

4 wireless [ˋwaɪrlɪs] *adj.* 無線的，無線電的

The spy sent the news by wireless telegraph.
間諜用無線電報把消息傳出。

5 whirlwind　[ˋhwɝ͵wɪnd]　*n.*　旋風　*adj.*　旋風般的

A whirlwind attacked the village.

旋風襲擊了這座村莊。

6 enrich　[ɪnˋrɪtʃ]　*vt.*　使富裕；使豐富

The popularity of the new products has enriched the owners.

新產品的成功使店主們富裕起來。

Reading can enrich our life.

閱讀可豐富生活。

7 arouse　[əˋraʊz]　*vt.*　喚醒；引起；激起

The orphan's sufferings aroused our sympathy.

孤兒的苦難引起了我們的同情。

The subject has aroused a lot of attention.

這事已引發許多關注。

8 endless　[ˋɛndlɪs]　*adj.*　無止境的

The couple used to have endless arguments about education.

這對夫婦對教育有無盡的爭執。

9 outstretched　[͵aʊtˋstrɛtʃt]　*adj.*　伸開的，擴張的，延伸的

The girl ran up to her parents' outstretched arms.

小女孩跑向父母伸出的手臂。

outstretched fingers 手指張開

10 seduce　[sɪˋdjus]　*v.*　勾引；誘惑

主題 4

Sandra was seduced into leaving the company by the higher pay elsewhere.

其他地方以更優厚的薪金待遇誘使珊卓離開了公司。

11 **kindred** [ˋkɪndrɪd] *n.* 家屬，親戚關係 *adj.* 同類的

Most of his kindred live in Australia.

他的親戚大部分住在澳洲。

Linda and I are kindred spirits.

琳達和我志趣相投。

12 **membership** [ˋmɛmbə͵ʃɪp] *n.* 成員資格；會員人數

Ethan applied for membership to the society.

伊森申請該協會的會員資格。

13 **dialogue** [ˋdaɪə͵lɔg] *n.* 對話，對白

Finally there can be a reasonable dialogue between the two leaders.

二位領袖最後終於能理智地進行對話了。

14 **inquire** [ɪnˋkwaɪr] *vt.* 打聽，詢問；調查

The detective will inquire into the murder case.

偵探將調查這起謀殺案。

I am calling to inquire about your advertisement in the newspaper.

我是打來詢問有關你們在報上登的廣告。

15 **respond** [rɪˋspɑnd] *vi.* 作答；回應

Peter invited Cathy to the party, but she did not respond.
彼得邀請凱西去派對，但她未作回答。

16 response　[rɪ`spɑns]　*n.*　作答，回答；回應

Millions of people donate in response to the famine appeal.
千百萬人回應救災呼籲而捐款。

an emotional response 情緒反應

17 interpret　[ɪn`tɜprɪt]　*vt.*　解釋，說明；口譯

I didn't presume to interpret the idea.
我不敢對這想法妄加解釋。

18 submit　[səb`mɪt]　*vt.*　使服從；提交　*vi.*　屈從

The suspect refused to submit to the court's judgment.
嫌犯不服法院判決。

All application letters have to be submitted by Friday.
所有的申請書都必須在星期五前遞交。

主題 4

19 publish　[`pʌblɪʃ]　*vt.*　*vi.*　出版；發行

The second edition has been published last week.
第二版在上星期已出版。

publishing house 出版社

20 lurk　[lɜk]　*vi.*　潛伏，埋伏

She didn't see the figure lurking behind the trees.
她沒看見在樹後躲藏的人。

lurk in the shadows 隱藏

21 **idleness** [ˈaɪdḷnɪs] *n.* 懶惰；賦閒無事

Mr. Lee cannot afford leaving the farm idle.

李先生無法負擔農田閒置的代價。

idle bone 懶骨頭

22 **intoxicate** [ɪnˈtɑksəˌket] *vt.* 使喝醉，陶醉

The driver was charged with driving while intoxicated.

駕駛因酒駕而被起訴。

23 **craze** [krez] *n.* 狂熱，大流行

The girls had a craze for collecting Barbie dolls.

那些女孩子們熱衷於收集芭比娃娃。

【同】 fashion, vogue, rage

24 **rely** [rɪˈlaɪ] *vi.* 依賴，依靠；信賴

We are relying on your decision.

我們相信你的判斷。

25 **impose** [ɪmˈpoz] *vi.* 利用；欺騙 *vt.* 徵稅；把……強加於

The greedy man knew he was imposed on.

貪心的男人知道自己上了當。

The government imposes a heavy tax on the luxury home.

政府對豪宅課重稅。

impose a burden on sb. 把負擔強加於某人……

26 **protection** [prəˈtɛkʃən] *n.* 保護，警戒

More and more people are aware of the importance of

environment protection.

愈來愈多人察覺環境保護的重要。

provide protection for 提供保護給……

27 regulate　　[`rɛgjə,let]　*vt.*　管理，控制；調整

A rule was announced to regulate the use of chemicals in vegetables.

一則規定管制蔬菜的化學藥物的使用。

regulate the temperature 控管溫度

28 movement　　[`muvmənt]　*n.*　動作，活動；移動

A movement was held by students to forbid smoking.

學生舉辦一場反對吸煙的運動。

political movement 政治運動

29 master　　[`mæstɚ]　*n.*　主人；能手；碩士　*vt.*　精通；控制

The dog is loyal to his master.

這條狗始終忠於它的主人。

The dialogue is a good way for mastering vocabulary.

對話是掌握詞彙的好方法。

主題 4

30 mode　　[mod]　*n.*　方式，樣式

July holds the western modes of thought.

茱莉持洋化思想。

This department has an efficient mode of operation.

這部門有一套有效的運作模式。

Games 遊戲

 Track 41

1 pastime [`pæs,taɪm] *n.* 消遣，娛樂

My brother's favorite pastime is fishing.

我弟弟最喜歡的娛樂是釣魚。

2 restless [`rɛstlɪs] *adj.* 不安定的，焦慮的

Jenny got restless and was going to move on after two weeks in Tokyo.

待在東京二個禮拜，珍妮開始煩躁準備動身離開。

restless night 輾轉難眠

3 entice [ɪn`taɪs] *vt.* 慫恿，引誘

The girl was enticed to run away from home.

這個女孩被引誘逃家。

【同】lure, tempt

4 woo [wu] *vt.* 向（女人）求愛，爭取……的支援

The guy is wooing my friend.

那個男人在追我的朋友。

woo fame and fortune 爭名奪利

5 quest [kwɛst] *vt.* 尋找 *vi.* 追求

We journeyed to the Snow Mountains in quest of pure salt.

他們旅行至雪山尋找純鹽。

quest for truth 追尋真理

6 phantom [ˋfæntəm] *n.* 鬼怪，幽靈，幻象 *adj.* 幽靈似的；有名無實的

I stared at Lillian for a while as if she were a phantom.

我盯著麗莉安看了一會兒，好像她是一個幽靈。

The police discovered a phantom company established for processing the profit of drugs.

警方發現一家經手毒品利益的空殼公司。

7 warrior [ˋwɔrɪə] *n.* 武士；鬥士

The brave warrior shot an arrow at his opponent.

那個勇士對準對手射了一箭。

8 lusty [ˋlʌstɪ] *adj.* 精力充沛的

Rita has a strong and lusty son.

芮塔有一個體格健壯精力充沛的兒子。

lusty singing 宏亮的歌聲

9 comrade [ˋkɑmræd] *n.* 同志，伙伴

Some comrades were killed in the war.

有些戰友在戰爭中被殺。

comrade in arms 戰友

10 excitement [ɪkˋsaɪtmənt] *n.* 刺激，興奮

主題 4

The report caused excitement among physicists.

這份研究報告讓物理學家們興奮。

flushed excitement 激動不已

11 **rapt** [ræpt] *adj.* 專注的

Students listen to their teacher with rapt attention.

學生們專心地聽著老師說話。

the rapt expression of his face 他臉上專注的表情

12 **vision** [ˋvɪʒən] *n.* 視力；眼光，想像力

The doctor tried to help the child with the problem of poor vision.

醫生試著幫助有視力問題的孩子。

tunnel vision 目光狹窄

13 **stare** [stɛr] *vi.* *vt.* 盯，凝視

Don't stare at me like that.

不要那樣盯著看我。

14 **hitherto** [ˏhɪðɚˋtu] *adv.* 迄今，到目前為止

There is a species of birds hitherto unknown in the East.

有種在東部的鳥類至今不為人知。

15 **wholesome** [ˋholsəm] *adj.* 有益健康的；有益身心的

Milk is a wholesome food.

牛奶是一種有益於健康的食品。

【同】healthy

【反】harmful

16 **mystery**　[ˋmɪstərɪ]　*n.*　謎，偵探小說

That murder is wrapped in mystery.

那件兇殺籠罩在神秘的氣氛之中。

17 **tempt**　[tɛmpt]　*vt.*　引誘，誘惑，勸誘

The game is designed tempt young men to study math.

這遊戲是被設計用來吸引年輕人學習數學。

tempt fate 試探命運

18 **conspiracy**　[kənˋspɪrəsɪ]　*n.*　陰謀

The politician is a party to the conspiracy.

政客參與了那次陰謀。

conspiracy theory 陰謀論

19 **sacrifice**　[ˋsækrə͵faɪs]　*n.* *vt.*　犧牲；獻祭

A lamb was offered up as a sacrifice to the God.

一隻羔羊被犧牲當作祭天的獻祭。

Mothers always sacrifice themselves for their children.

母親總為小孩犧牲。

self-sacrifice 自我犧牲

20 **vicious**　[ˋvɪʃəs]　*adj.*　邪惡的；惡性的

Stay away from the stray dog, he can be vicious.

離那隻流浪狗遠一點，牠很兇。

主題 4

21 **wickedness** [ˋwɪkɪdnɪs] *n.* 邪惡，不正；惡意，壞心眼

May God wash me thoroughly from my wickedness.
願上帝洗淨我的邪惡。

22 **perceive** [pɚˋsiv] *vt.* 察覺，發覺；理解

I perceived a change in his behavior.
我發覺他的行為有些變化。

23 **difficult** [ˋdɪfəˏkəlt] *adj.* 困難的；難對付的

It's difficult for Mandy to cook.
煮飯對於曼蒂來說是難的。
difficult questions 困難的問題

24 **circumstance** [ˋsɝkəmˏstæns] *n.* 情況，條件；境遇

Drivers can only run a red light under certain
circumstances.
在某些特別情況下，駕駛才能闖紅燈。
economic circumstance 經濟條件

25 **spoil** [spɔɪl] *vt.* 損壞，糟蹋；寵壞

A fond mother may spoil her child.
溺愛的母親可能會寵壞她的孩子。
The entire meadows are spoiled by trash.
整個草坪都被垃圾破壞。
spoil oneself 放縱自己

26 **outrun** [aʊtˋrʌn] *vt.* 超過，逃脫

The live concert outran its time.

這現場音樂會超過了預定時間。

The robber outran the police chasing after him.

搶匪逃脫警察的追捕。

27 **overtake** [ˌovə·ˋtek] *vt.* 追上，趕上；壓倒

The little boy had to walk very fast to overtake his brother.

小男孩要走得很快才能趕上他哥哥。

28 **overthrow** [ˌovə·ˋθro] *vt.* 推翻 *n.* 推翻，瓦解

They were plotting the overthrow of the government.

他們正在策劃推翻政府。

The government was overthrown by the army.

政府被軍隊推翻。

29 **applause** [əˋplɔz] *n.* 喝彩；誇獎，稱讚

The economic reform was met with agreed applause.

經濟改革得到眾口一致的稱讚。

rapturous applause 熱情的掌聲

thunderous applause 如雷的掌聲

主題 4

30 **slumber** [ˋslʌmbə·] *vi.* 睡眠 *n.* 睡眠；沉睡狀態

The old lady slumbered away a hot afternoon.

老婦人以睡眠打發一個炎熱的下午。

slumber party（少女通霄閒聊的）睡衣晚會

Tech History 科技史

Track 42

1 **abacus** [`æbəkəs] *n.* 算盤

The abacus was used for calculating in ancient times.
算盤在古代用來計算。

2 **windmill** [`wɪnd,mɪl] *n.* 風車

Windmills can be used for producing electrical power.
風車可用來產生電力。

3 **loom** [lum] *n.* 織布機 *vi.* 隱約地出現

I don't know how to use a hand loom.
我不知道怎樣使用手工織布機。

loom up / out 隱約現身

loom on the horizon 即將出現

4 **telegraph** [`tɛlə,græf] *n.* 電報機；電報 *vi. vt.* 打電報（給）

Telegraph the doctor to come at once.
打電報通知醫生馬上來。

5 **telegram** [`tɛlə,græm] *n.* 電報

He has clapped a telegram for me.

他給我派了封電報。

6 bulb [bʌlb] *n.* 電燈泡；球狀物

This light bulb has gone.

這燈泡滅了。

tulip bulbs 鬱金香球莖

7 tube [tjub] *n.* 管；電子管，顯像管

Please suck on the tube to draw up the water.

請用管子把水吸上來。

test tube 試管

tube sock 無腳跟的短筒襪

a toilet roll tube 廁所的捲筒

8 cassette [kəˋsɛt] *n.* 盒式錄音帶；盒子

She bought a lot of cassettes when she was young.

她年輕時買了很多卡帶。

9 formerly [ˋfɔrməlɪ] *adv.* 以前，從前

The splendid hotel was formerly a palace.

這金碧輝煌的飯店之前是皇宮。

10 prosper [ˋprɑspɚ] *vi.* 繁榮

The nation is prospering under the lead of the new president.

在一個新總統的帶領下，這個國家正逐漸繁榮起來。

11 forsake [fəˋsek] *vt.* 遺棄，拋棄，摒絕

主題 **4**

Derek will never forsake his vegetarian principle.
德瑞克絕不摒棄吃素原則。

12 shift [ʃɪft] *vt. vi.* 替換，轉移 *n.* 轉換

Nelson's cheek flushed and soon shifted to a new subject.
尼爾森二頰脹紅，很快地轉換一個新的話題。

shift gear 改變方法

13 languish [ˈlæŋgwɪʃ] *vi.* 衰弱，變得消瘦

The flowers languished from lack of water.
花因缺水而枯萎。

The stock market continues to languish.
股市持續低迷。

languish in 因……長期受苦

14 inventor [ɪnˈvɛntɚ] *n.* 發明者；發明家

The machine was named after its inventor.
這機器的名字來自其發明者。

15 creator [krɪˈetɚ] *n.* 創建者

Creation supposes a creator.
有了創造者，才能有創造。

16 patent [ˈpætnt] *adj.* 專利的 *n.* 專利

The patent runs out in three years.
這項專利期限為 3 年。

They applied for a patent for their new product.

他們為新產品申請專利。

take out a patent 取得專利

17 preliminary [prɪ`lɪmə,nɛrɪ] *adj.* 預備的，初步的 *n.*
開端，初步

Kitty spent a long time on polite preliminaries in the party.
派對上，凱蒂花許多時間在客套上。

18 criticism [`krɪtə,sɪzəm] *n.* 批評；批判；評論

I accepted their criticism of my comments.
我接受了他們對我意見的批評。

harsh / severe criticism 嚴厲的批評

level criticism at sb. 批評某人

a storm of criticism 排山倒海而來的批評

19 pressure [`prɛʃə] *n.* 壓力；壓力；壓，按

The chief administrator is under pressure to resign.
主要的管理者在壓力下辭職。

blood pressure 血壓

20 overlook [,ovə`lʊk] *vt.* 眺望；看漏；寬容

Researchers overlooked the high risks involved.
研究者們忽略了暗含的高風險。

overlook sb.'s behavior 原諒某人的行為舉止

21 hardship [`hardʃɪp] *n.* 艱難，困苦

He is never afraid of hardship.

主題 **4**

他從來不怕艱苦。

22 **obscure**　[əb`skjʊr]　*adj.*　陰暗的；模糊的；無名的

The detail of the writer's life remains obscure.

這個作家生活的詳情還是不為人知。

an obscure poem 沒沒無聞的詩

23 **doom**　[dum]　*n.*　命運，毀滅　*vt.*　註定

The company was doomed to bankruptcy.

這公司注定破產。

A sense of doom gripped the soldier.

大難臨頭的感覺縈繞著士兵。

doom to extinction 注定絕種

24 **discern**　[dɪ`zɝn]　*vt.*　看出，辨出；辨別

Candidates are eager to discern how much public support there was.

候選人急切的想知道大眾的支持度。

discern from 從……辨別

25 **fortify**　[`fɔrtə,faɪ]　*vt.*　增強

The legislator's position was fortified by election successes.

立委的地位因勝選而更穩固。

【同】strengthen, reinforce

26 **impel**　[ɪm`pɛl]　*vt.*　推進，驅使

The lack of democracy impelled the crowd to fight for

political rights.

不民主驅使群眾為政治權而戰。

【同】urge, advance, expedite

【反】restrain

27 **progressive** [prəˈgrɛsɪv] *adj.* 進步的；向前進的

He is the most progressive writer of those times.

他是那個時代最進步的作家。

28 **surge** [sɝdʒ] *n. vi.* 波濤洶湧，波動；蜂擁而到

A surge of customers broke through the fence.

洶湧而來的顧客衝破了籬笆。

The students surged forward to the bus.

學生們蜂擁靠近公車。

29 **billow** [ˈbɪlo] *n.* 巨浪 *vi.* 波浪似的起伏

Billows of clouds were appearing from the west.

波狀雲朵正從西邊出現。

Smoke billowed from the factory.

煙從工廠湧出。

主題 4

30 **revolution** [ˌrɛvəˈluʃən] *n.* 革命；旋轉，繞轉

These people go around preaching revolution.

這些人到處宣揚革命。

sexual revolution 性別革命

social revolution 社會革命

industrial revolution 工業革命

Earth 地球

Track 43

1 **earth** [ɝθ] *n.* 地球

The moon goes around the earth.

月亮繞著地球轉。

in the earth 在土裡

on earth 究竟，到底，全世界，世界上

earth mother 大地之母

2 **dimension** [dɪˋmɛnʃən] *n.* 尺寸；面積；方面

What are the dimensions of the box?

這個盒子的尺寸是多少？

political dimension 政治面

social dimension 經濟面

3 **massive** [ˋmæsɪv] *adj.* 粗大的；大而重的

The church is supported by massive columns.

此教堂由粗大的柱子支撐。

a massive stroke 嚴重的中風

4 **round** [raʊnd] *prep.* 圍（繞）著

My family sat round the table.

我的家人圍餐桌坐著。

round up 把⋯⋯趕到一起，使聚攏
round-trip 往返旅行，雙程旅行

5 **orb** [ɔrb] *n.* 球，天體，圓形物
The glowing orb of the sun rises from the east every day.
閃耀的太陽每天從東方升起。

6 **sphere** [sfɪr] *n.* 球，圓體；範圍
Exchanges with other countries in the cultural sphere are a good way to show friendship.
與他國作文化方面的交流是展現友誼好方式。

7 **hemisphere** [`hɛməs,fɪr] *n.* 半球；半球地圖
In the northern hemisphere, spring is in March and April.
在北半球，春季是三月和四月。
the Southern hemisphere 南半球

主題 4

8 **axis** [`æksɪs] *n.* 軸，軸線；第二頸椎
The Earth rotates on an axis between the south and north poles.
地球繞著南、北極軸線旋轉。

9 **traverse** [`trævɚs] *vt.* 橫越，橫切，橫斷
Searching lights traversed the ocean.
探照燈掃過海面。
The sportier spent one minute to traverse the gym.
運動員花一分中橫越體運場。

10 northern [`nɔrðə·n] *adj.* 北方的，北部的

The Confederacy was defeated by the northern states.

南部邦聯被北方打敗了。

11 southward [`saʊθwə·d] *adv.* 向南方地 *adj.* 南方的

The sailors followed the coast southward.

水手們沿著海岸向南行進。

the southward route to 往……南方航線

12 equator [ɪ`kwetə·] *n.* 赤道，天球赤道

Singapore is near the equator.

新加坡位於赤道附近。

on the equator 赤道上

13 tropic [`trɑpɪk] *n.* 熱帶地區；回歸線

My country is located to the south of the Tropic of Cancer.

我的國家在北回歸線的南面。

the tropical rain forest 熱帶雨林

14 pole [pol] *n.* 杆；柱

The cabin was built with poles covered with grass mats.

這小屋是用其上面蓋草蓆的柱子建成的。

the South Pole 南極

the North Pole 北極

the Pole Star 北極星

15 region [`ridʒən] *n.* 地區，地帶；領域

Are most of the houses located in the south central region?

大部分的房子都在南部中心地區嗎？

The Red Cross is making efforts to offer rescue to the region.

紅十字會正努力給那地區提供救援。

the coastal region 海域

16 zone [zon] *n.* 地區，區域，範圍

The western part of the country has become a war zone.

這國家的西部已變成戰區。

time zone 時區

17 continent [ˋkɑntənənt] *n.* 大陸；洲

Antarctica is a continent centered roughly on the South Pole.

南極洲是一片大致以南極為中心的大陸。

18 peninsula [pəˋnɪnsələ] *n.* 半島

Their villa is located on the bottom of the peninsula.

他們的度假別墅位於半島的末端。

19 campo [ˋkæmpo] *n.* 平野，平原

A herd of cattle were running across the campo.

一大群牛正橫越草原。

20 evergreen [ˋɛvɚˏgrin] *n.* 常綠樹，常綠植物 *adj.* 長綠的，長青的

主題 **4**

Spruce and pine are evergreen trees.
雲杉和松樹都是常綠樹木。

21 grassy [ˋgræsɪ] *adj.* 草多的；草似的
Those children slid down the grassy hill.
我們順著草丘滑下去。

22 sod [sɑd] *n.* 草地，草坪，故鄉；討厭鬼
The sports field was covered with sod.
體育場上覆蓋著草皮。
sod all 甚麼也沒有
be a sod 難應付
not give a sod 毫不關心

23 dell [dɛl] *n.* 小谷，小溪谷
Many flowers grew on both sides of the dell.
溪谷的兩岸有許多花。

24 serene [səˋrin] *adj.* 寧靜的，沉著的，安詳的，晴朗的
The attack happened in a serene winter night.
攻擊發生在一個寧靜的冬夜。

25 womb [wum] *n.* 子宮，發源地
The scheme lies in the womb of time.
此計畫在醞釀中。
A mother's health can influence the baby in the womb.
媽媽的健康會影響子宮裡的嬰兒。

26 glance [glæns] *vi.* 看一下 *n.* 一瞥

Lucy gave Rick an adoring glance.

露西向瑞克投以愛慕的一瞥。

I glanced at the clock, and it was almost midnight.

我看了鐘一眼，幾乎半夜了。

27 moon [mun] *n.* 月球，月亮；衛星

The moon goes around the earth.

月亮繞著地球轉。

28 bare [bɛr] *adj.* 赤裸的；僅僅的

He ran out of the house with bare feet when it was on fire.

火災發生時，他光著腳跑出房子。

the bare facts 沒有細節的陳述

29 parch [pɑrtʃ] *v.* 烘，烤

The fierce sun parched the grassland.

灼熱的陽光炙烤著這片草地。

Those plants parched after the noon.

那些植物在正午後被曬乾枯了。

主題 4

30 perish [ˋpɛrɪʃ] *vi.* 死亡，夭折；枯萎

Many people perished when the boat went down.

船翻了，許多人死了。

perish the thought 打消念頭

Unit
08

Geography 地理

Track 44

1 geography ［ˋdʒɪˋɑgrəfɪ］ *n.* 地理，地理學

How's the new geography teacher?
新的地理老師怎麼樣？

2 meridian ［məˋrɪdɪən］ *n.* 子午線，經線，頂點

Berlin is on the same meridian with Rome.
柏霖和羅馬在同一經線上。

the prime medridian 本初子午線
the meridian（太陽等天體對地面而言）最高點

3 longitude ［ˋlɑndʒəˋtjud］ *n.* 經線，經度

The city lies at longitude 20° W.
這城市位於西經二十度。

4 latitude ［ˋlætə,tjud］ *n.* 緯度；黃緯；自由

These migratory birds breed in southern latitudes.
候鳥在南緯地區繁殖。

considerable latitude 極大的自由

5 midway ［ˋmɪdwe］ *n.* *adv.* 中途，中間

The market is midway between these two villages.

在這兩個村的中間有個市集。

Michelle quit midway through her pregnancy.

米雪兒在懷孕中期辭職。

6 arctic [`ɑrktɪk] *adj.* 北極的；截然對立的 *n.* 北極

Eskimos live in the Arctic.

愛斯基摩人生活在北極。

Arctic Ocean 北極洋

Arctic Circle 北極圈

7 polar [`polɚ] *adj.* 南（北）極的；極性的

The polar bears are endangered.

北極熊快絕種了。

The polar ice caps begin to melt because of global warming.

極地冰帽因全球暖化開始融化。

8 explorer [ɪk`splorɚ] *n.* 探險家，探測者

Allen is an Arctic explorer.

艾倫是個極地探險家。

主題 4

9 observation [ˌɑbzɚ`veʃən] *n.* 注意；觀察；觀察力

She is under observation.

她被監視。

The patient spent a week under close observation in hospital.

這病患花了一星期在醫院作密切的觀察。

direct observation 直接觀察

10 **ascend** 　[əˋsɛnd]　*vi.* 　*vt.* 　攀登，登高；追溯

My ancestors ascend to the 17th century.

我的祖先可上溯到十七世紀。

Mountain-climbers slowly ascended up the steep hill.

登山客慢慢地攀上陡峭的山丘。

ascend the throne 登上王位

11 **aloft** 　[əˋlɔft]　*adv.* 　在高處，在上

The balloons went aloft.

氣球升向天空。

hold/bear sth. aloft 把……高舉

12 **compass** 　[ˋkʌmpəs]　*n.* 　羅盤，指南針；圓規

The compass was invented by Chinese.

羅盤是中國人發明的。

13 **orient** 　[ˋorɪənt]　*n.* 　東方；亞洲，遠東

Ian is a dab hand at the art of the Orient.

伊恩是東方藝術的行家。

oriental cuisine 東方菜餚

14 **enchantment** 　[ɪnˋtʃæntmənt]　*n.* 　著魔，喜悅

Vincent is enjoying the enchantment of poetry.

文森正享受詩的魔力。

15 **dusk** 　[dʌsk]　*n.* 　薄暮，黃昏，幽暗

As dusk fell, owls appeared in the forest.

黑夜來臨時貓頭鷹就在森林裡出現。

16 **highland** [`haɪlənd] *n.* 高地，丘陵地帶 *adj.* 高地的

Some villages in the highlands are connected by telegram.

一些在高地的村落是藉由電報來聯繫。

Highland fling 蘇格蘭高地舞

17 **lowland** [`loland] *n.* 低地，蘇格東南部的低地 *adj.*
低地的

He lives in the Scottish lowlands.

他住在蘇格蘭低地。

Some kinds of plants are only found in lowland areas.

有些植物只在低地地區可找到。

18 **heath** [hiθ] *n.* 荒地

She lost her way in the heath.

她在荒地裡迷了路。

Heath Robinson 太過精巧不合實用的

19 **barren** [`bærən] *adj.* 貧瘠的；不妊的；無趣的

This sea was a barren dessert one hundred years ago.

這海一百年前是一片荒蕪的沙漠。

The stadium is just a barren concrete building.

這體育館只是一棟不吸引目光的建築物。

20 **knoll** [nol] *n.* 小圓丘

There is a grassy knoll behind the house.

主題 4

房子後面有一個綠草如茵的土墩。

21 cavern [ˈkævɚn] *n.* 大洞穴

The criminal hid himself in the dark cavern.

罪犯藏身黑暗的洞穴。

22 cavity [ˈkævətɪ] *n.* 洞，穴，空腔

They dig a cavity in the earth.

他們挖了一個地下洞穴。

The cook put the spices inside the body cavity of the fish.

廚師把香料放進魚身體裡。

cavity wall 空心牆

23 limestone [ˈlaɪmˌston] *n.* 石灰石

Stalactite is formed by water that drips down from limestone.

鐘乳石是由從石灰石滴下的水所形成。

24 hillside [ˈhɪlˌsaɪd] *n.* （小山）山腰，山坡

The path narrows as you climb the hillside.

沿著山坡往上爬時，那條小徑越來越窄。

steep hillside 陡峭的山坡

25 cliff [klɪf] *n.* 懸崖，峭壁

You can climb up with the holds on the cliff face.

你可藉著峭壁正面可供手攀或腳踏的地方往上爬。

Stay away from the edge of the cliff.

遠離懸崖邊。

26 crag [kræg] *n.* 懸崖，峭壁

The insane woman jumped off the crag.

那個瘋了的女人跳下了懸崖。

27 summit [`sʌmɪt] *n.* 頂點，最高點；極度

The rescue team has reached the summit of Jade Mountain.

救難隊已到達玉山山頂。

28 cascade [kæs`ked] *n.* 小瀑布；瀑布狀的東西

A cascade of blonde hair fell down from her shoulders.

一頭金髮從她肩上垂下。

29 torrent [`tɔrənt] *n.* 奔流，激流，洪流

The water poured down the mountain in torrents.

洪水從山上奔流而下。

After the heavy rain, the river is a very violent torrent.

大雨後河水奔流。

主題 4

30 cataract [`kætə,rækt] *n.* 大瀑布，奔流，洪水，白內障

Cataracts of rain flooded this area.

傾盆大雨使這區淹水。

The river fell in a succession of spectacular cataracts.

這小河以一道壯觀的奔流瀉下。

remove a cataract 移除白內障

Biology 生物學

1　delta　　[ˋdɛltə]　*n.*　（河流的）三角洲

There are fertile fields in the Yangtze River Delta.

長江三角洲土地肥沃。

2　marsh　　[marʃ]　*n.*　沼澤地，濕地

The ground had become a marsh due to the constant rain.

那塊地因不斷的降雨而變成沼澤。

marsh gas 沼氣

3　stork　　[stɔrk]　*n.*　鸛

In ancient times, the white stork is a supposed bringer of new-born babies.

白鶴在古代是帶來新生命的象徵。

4　locust　　[ˋlokəst]　*n.*　蝗蟲

A locust is a kind of insect pest.

蝗蟲是一種害蟲。

migratory locust 遷徙性蝗蟲

5　rare　　[rɛr]　*adj.*　稀薄的；稀有的

A diamond is a rare jewel.

鑽石是罕見的珠寶。

It's rare for Jane to miss a day at school.

珍一天沒上學是罕見的。

6　conceive　[kən`siv]　*vt.*　設想，以為；懷孕

Louise was told by the doctor she couldn't conceive.

醫生告訴露薏絲她無法懷孕。

My father can't conceive of a supper without fish.

我父親無法想像沒有魚可吃的晚餐。

ill-conceived 計劃不周的

7　fertilize　[`fɝt!,aɪz]　*vt.*　使受精

An egg fertilized by the sperm will become an embryo.

受精卵會變成胚胎。

8　membrane　[`mɛmbren]　*n.*　薄膜，細胞膜

Loud noise will damage the membrane in the ear.

太大的噪音會危害耳膜。

主題 **4**

9　larva　[`lɑrvə]　*n.*　（昆蟲的）幼蟲

This worm is the larva of a butterfly.

這蟲子是蝴蝶的幼蟲。

10　cell　[sɛl]　*n.*　細胞；單人囚房

There are red blood cells, white blood cells and platelets in human's blood.

人體的血液裡有紅血球、白血球和血小板。

The criminal was in prisoned in a cell.
罪犯被關在單人牢房。

11 embryo [ˈɛmbrɪ͵o] *n.* 胚胎

The plans are still in embryo.
計畫仍在醞釀中。

The embryo will grow into a fetus in a few weeks.
胚胎在幾個星期後會發育成胎兒。

embryo transfer 胚胎植入

12 selection [səˈlɛkʃən] *n.* 選擇，挑選；精選物

The selection of our new leader will start in five minutes.
新班長的選拔會在五分鐘後開始。

natural selection 天擇

13 zoological [͵zoəˈlɑdʒɪkḷ] *adj.* 動物學的

The zoological specimens room is upstairs.
動物標本室在樓上。

zoological research 動物學研究

zoological classification 動物分類法

14 instinct [ˈɪnstɪŋkt] *n.* 本能；直覺；生性

Most animals have a natural instinct for survival.
大部分的動物有生存的本能。

sexual instinct 性別本能

15　**instinctive**　[ɪnˋstɪŋktɪv]　*adj.*　本能的

Flying is instinctive in birds.

鳥類飛行出於本能。

16　**controversy**　[ˋkɑntrəˌvɝsɪ]　*n.*　爭論，辯論，爭吵

There are some issues under controversy.

有一些議題仍在爭論。

provoke controversy 引發爭議

17　**distinguish**　[dɪˋstɪŋgwɪʃ]　*vt.*　區別，辨別，識別

The little boy can't distinguish right from wrong.

小男孩無法分辨對錯。

18　**dumb**　[dʌm]　*adj.*　啞的；無言的

Dumb dogs are dangerous.

【諺】不吠的狗最危險。

dumb show 默劇

主題 4

19　**mankind**　[ˋmænˌkaɪnd]　*n.*　人類

His life is a microcosm of the whole of mankind.

他的一生是全人類的縮影。

research for the benefit of all mankind 尋找全人類的福祉

20　**nameless**　[ˋnemlɪs]　*adj.*　無名的，匿名的，不可名狀的

The professor discovered some new and nameless insects.

教授發現了一些新的未命名的昆蟲。

21 vital [ˋvaɪt!] *adj.* 生命的，生機的

The heart is a vital organ to the human body.

心臟是人類身體必需的器官。

play a vital role in sth. 在……裡扮演重要角色

vital element 重要的元素

22 rear [rɪr] *v.* 撫養，培養 *n.* 後部，後面；背面

This school is a good place rear young children.

這學校是個培育小孩的好地方。

To the rear of the hut is a forest land.

房子後面是一塊林地。

rear its ugly head 無法忽視

23 fill [fɪl] *vt.* 裝滿，盛滿；占滿

Please fill the bucket with water.

請把桶子裝滿水。

24 carbohydrate [ˌkɑrbəˋhaɪdret] *n.* 碳水化合物

Carbohydrates provide heat and energy to our body.

碳水化合物給我們的身體提供熱量和能量。

25 digest [daɪˋdʒɛst] *vt.* 消化，領悟 *vi.* 消化

This rich food doesn't digest easily.

這種油膩的食物不易消化。

I struggle to digest the poem.

我努力的了解這首詩。

26 **bacteria** [bæk'tɪərɪə] *n.* 細菌

Most bacteria are too small to see with the naked eye.
大部分的細菌太小，肉眼看不見。
bacterium 為細菌複數

27 **pore** [por] *n.* 毛孔，氣孔，細孔

Pores blocked with dirt and oil will become pimples.
被髒汙及油脂阻塞的毛孔會變成青春痘。

28 **infect** [ɪn'fɛkt] *vt.* 使受影響，傳染

Many refugees in Africa are infected with HIV.
非洲許多難民感染愛滋病病毒。

29 **germ** [dʒɝm] *n.* 細菌；微生物；起點

Hands contain germs invisible to the naked eye.
手有肉眼看不見的細菌。
The germ of a fiction begins to form in Rowling's mind.
小說的起點開始在羅琳心中生根。
the germ of a theory 理論的萌芽

主題 4

30 **rot** [rɑt] *vi. vt.* （使）腐爛

The fish will rot if it isn't kept cool.
魚如果不冷藏就會腐敗。
Sweets will rot your teeth.
甜食會蛀蝕牙齒。

Physics 物理學

Track 46

1 theory   [ˋθɪərɪ]   *n.*   理論；原理

He at last published his new theory in 1688.

終於在一六八八年他發表了他的新理論。

2 prove   [pruv]   *vt.*   證明，證實

I have to prove her innocence.

我必須證實她的無辜。

3 implement   [ˋɪmpləmənt]   *n.*   工具，服裝   *vt.*   貫徹；實施

It is not proper to implement a plan by force.

強迫實施一項計畫不適當。

The changes of the taxation system will be implemented next month.

稅徵制度的改變將於下個月執行。

4 logic   [ˋlɑdʒɪk]   *n.*   邏輯，推理；邏輯性

It's hard to accept his logic.

接受他的邏輯是難的。

commercial logic 商業操作邏輯

5 ingenuity [ˌɪndʒəˋnuətɪ] *n.* 機靈；巧妙

I had been surprised by their ingenuity.
我對他們的足智多謀感到驚訝。
the ingenuity of a plan 計畫之巧妙

6 particle [ˋpɑrtɪk!] *n.* 粒子，微粒；極小量

There is not a particle of constructive opinions in his speech.
他說的話沒有一點建設性意見。
dust particles 微塵粒子
particle physics 粒子物理學

7 pulsate [ˋpʌlˏset] *vi.* 有規律的振動

The water seemed to pulsate with a spray of sunlight.
水似乎隨著陽光的照射而顫動。

8 impulse [ˋɪmpʌls] *n.* 推動，衝力；衝動

My wife bought the diamond on an impulse.
我太太一時衝動買下了那鑽石。
impulse buying 衝動購買
a sudden impulse to laugh 突然想笑的衝動

9 circuit [ˋsɝkɪt] *n.* 電路；環行；巡行

There are two breakers in this circuit.
這個電路裡面使用了兩個斷路器。

主題 4

10 **direct** [də`rɛkt] *vt.* 指導 *adj.* 直接的

Steven Spielberg directed the film.

史帝芬‧史匹柏導演這部電影。

11 **measurement** [`mɛʒəmənt] *n.* 衡量，測量；尺寸

Take measurements of the bathroom before you buy a new bathtub.

在你買新浴缸前要先測量浴室大小。

12 **busily** [`bɪzḷɪ] *adv.* 忙碌地

These students are answering the test paper busily.

這些學生正忙著在考試卷上作答。

13 **motionless** [`moʃənlɪs] *adj.* 不動的，靜止的

Scott remained motionless when the earthquake happened.

地震發生時，史考特一動也不動。

14 **suspend** [sə`spɛnd] *vt.* 吊，懸；推遲

Such fine particles suspend readily in air.

這種微粒極易懸浮在空中。

Sales of cars will be suspended until the tests are completed.

車子的銷售要延緩至測試都完成。

15 **could** [kʊd] *aux.* （can 的過去式）

Could I smoke here?

我可以在這裡抽煙嗎？

16 perchance [pɚˋtʃæns] *adv.* 偶然地；或許

Perchance Peter is not who he says he is.

或許彼得不是他自己說的那種人。

17 transient [ˋtrænʃənt] *adj.* 短暫的，轉瞬即逝的

His feeling of sadness was transient.

他傷心的心情一會兒就過去了。

transient fashions 短暫的流行

a transient population 短暫居留的人口

【反】permanent, eternal

18 transistor [trænˋzɪstɚ] *n.* 電晶體

A transistor is a small piece of electronic equipment that controls the flow of electricity.

電晶體是一小片電子設備，它能控制電流。

19 condenser [kənˋdɛnsɚ] *n.* 凝結器，冷凝器，冷卻器

A car engine will be equipped with a condenser.

車子引擎會裝置冷卻器。

主題 4

20 definite [ˋdɛfənɪt] *adj.* 明確的；肯定的

We can't say anything definite yet.

我們還不能肯定地說什麼。

21 tremendous　[trɪ`mɛndəs]　*adj.*　極大的，非常的

The tremendous explosion startled the crowd.

那極大的爆炸驚嚇到群眾。

This project may take us a tremendous amount of time.

這計畫也許會花掉我們許多時間。

tremendous support 壓倒性的支持

22 uproar　[`ʌp,ror]　*n.*　騷動，擾亂；喧囂

The room was in uproar, with babies crying.

這房間因嬰兒的哭聲而吵鬧。

The film caused an uproar in China.

這部電影在中國引起騷動。

23 echo　[`ɛko]　*vi.*　反射（聲音等）發聲回響　*n.*　回音

The station echoed with the wailing of fire-engine sirens.

車站裡回響著火車汽笛的尖嘯聲。

The woof echoed back from the forest.

吠聲在森林裡回響。

24 subsequent　[`sʌbsɪ,kwɛnt]　*adj.*　隨後的，後來的

The tradition was passed on to the subsequent generations.

這傳統傳承給接下的的世代。

25 conservation　[,kɑnsə`veʃən]　*n.*　保存，保護；守恆

Who discovered energy conservation?

誰發現了能量守恆？

26 core　　[kor]　　*n.*　　果實的心，核心

The core of his appeal is freedom of speech.

他要求的核心是言論自由。

Remove the cores and bake the pears for thirty minutes.

去除果核，把西洋梨烤三十分鐘。

27 gravity　　[ˋgrævətɪ]　　*n.*　　重力，引力；嚴重性

The leaves fell down the tree by gravity.

樹葉在重力作用下掉落。

You could not escape from their gravity of the situation.

你不能逃避他們對情況的擔心。

28 constant　　[ˋkɑnstənt]　　*adj.*　　經常的；永恆的

The children's constant laughter was irritating.

孩子們喋喋不休的笑聲使人心煩。

29 substance　　[ˋsʌbstəns]　　*n.*　　物質；實質；本旨

The emery is a hard metallic substance.

金剛砂是非常堅硬的金屬物質。

The wood was covered with a creamy substance.

木頭上覆蓋了乳脂似的物質。

主題 4

30 composition　　[ˌkɑmpəˋzɪʃən]　　*n.*　　組成，構成，結構

They examined the stone to find out its composition.

他們檢驗了這一石塊，想弄清它的構成成分。

written composition 書面作文

Chemistry 化學

Track 47

1 nature 　[`netʃɚ]　*n.*　大自然，自然界

To master life, you must know the laws of nature.

為了主宰生命，你必須知道自然法則。

nature energy 天然能源

2 aspire 　[ə`spaɪr]　*vi.*　熱望，立志

At that time, all serious musicians aspired to go to Vienna.

那時所有認真的音樂家都想去維也納。

3 organize 　[`ɔrgə,naɪz]　*vt.*　組織，編組

Service workers also have the right to organize.

服務性行業人員也有權組織工會。

4 periodical 　[,pɪrɪ`ɑdɪk!]　*n.*　期刊，雜誌

She kept sending her paper to the periodical.

她持續把自己的論文寄去期刊。

5 element 　[`ɛləmənt]　*n.*　元素；要素；成分

Oxygen is an element, while carbon dioxide is a compound.

氧是元素，而二氧化碳是化合物。

Generosity is an important element of his success.

慷慨是他成功的重要元素。

element of truth 一點道理

6 primary [`praɪ,mɛrɪ] *adj.* 最初的；基本的

The successful businessman only accepted the primary education off and on in his childhood.

這成功的商人小時候只斷斷續續地接受過初等教育。

primary election 初選

7 hydrogen [`haɪdrədʒən] *n.* 氫

Hydrogen is the lightest of all gases.

氫氣是所有氣體中最輕的。

hydrogen bomb 氫彈

8 potent [`potnt] *adj.* 強有力的

I was convinced by Kate's potent statement.

凱特那有力的說明把我說服了。

主題 4

9 combustion [kəm`bʌstʃən] *n.* 燃燒；氧化；騷動

Combustion is the process of burning.

氧化是燃燒的過程。

10 complement [`kɑmpləmənt] *vt.* 補充；與……相配
n. 補足（物）

This beer could be a nice complement to grilled dishes.

這啤酒會是燒烤菜餚的好配對。

The brown curtain complements the tan leather carpet.

棕色的窗簾與褐色地毯相配。

11 **compound** [kɑmˋpaʊnd] *n.* 化合物；複合詞

Air is a mixture of gases, not a compound.
空氣是氣體的混合物，不是化合物。

12 **commence** [kəˋmɛns] *vt.* *vi.* 開始

The house commenced burning at midnight.
房子從午夜開始燃燒。

The course commences with an introduction of art history.
這課程從藝術史的介紹開始。

13 **experiment** [ɪkˋspɛrəmənt] *n.* 實驗；試驗

The researchers are doing a chemical experiment.
研究者們正在做化學實驗。

carry out an experiment 完成實驗

14 **microscope** [ˋmaɪkrə͵skop] *n.* 顯微鏡

Each object was examined through a microscope.
每個物體都經由顯微鏡檢查。

under a microscope 在顯微鏡下

15 **accurate** [ˋækjərɪt] *adj.* 準確的，正確無誤的

The news was accurate.
這則新聞是準確的。

16 purity　[ˋpjʊrətɪ]　*n.*　純淨；純潔；純度

Chinese people consider the lotus as a symbol of purity.

中國人把蓮花看作是純潔的象徵。

spiritual purity 心靈的純淨

17 eliminate　[ɪˋlɪmə͵net]　*vt.*　消滅，消除，排除

Their team was eliminated in the first round.

他們隊在第一輪就被淘汰了。

18 absorption　[əbˋsɔrpʃən]　*n.*　吸收；專注

I highly praise his complete absorption in his work.

我極度推崇他對工作的極端專注。

19 reduction　[rɪˋdʌkʃən]　*n.*　減少，減小，縮減

The minster announced a slight reduction in the price of oil.

部長宣布石油價錢小幅調降。

20 rigour　[ˋrɪgɚ]　*n.*　嚴格，嚴厲，苛刻，精確，嚴密

That guy deserves to be punished within the full rigour of the law.

那男人應該受到法律最嚴厲的懲罰。

21 conclude　[kənˋklud]　*vt.*　*vi.*　結束，斷定

The professor concluded that the nuclear power plant should be closed immediately.

教授斷定和電廠應馬上關閉。

主題 4

22 **agree** [əˋgri] *vt.* *vi.* 同意，贊成

Do you agree with me about the need for more schools?

關於多建一些學校一事，你同意我的意見嗎？

agree with sb. 同意某人的意見

agree on (upon)（對事情）意見一致

23 **achievement** [əˋtʃivmənt] *n.* 完成；成就，成績

The coach tried to celebrate the achievement of his players.

教練想為球員的成績慶祝。

a sense of achievement 成就感

24 **official** [əˋfɪʃəl] *adj.* 官方的，正式的

The official statistics about the divorce rate is shown in the report.

有關離婚率的官方數據顯示在報告上。

25 **eminent** [ˋɛmənənt] *adj.* 著名的、顯著的

Nathan is an eminent lawyer.

那森是一位著名的律師。

26 **rebuke** [rɪˋbjuk] *vt.* *n.* 指責，非難，斥責

She chafes at the rebuke.

她對於指責感到惱怒。

I receive a stern rebuke from my mother.

我受到母親嚴厲的斥責。

27 intense [ɪnˋtɛns] *adj.* 強烈的；緊張的

The intense heat dried up the pool.

酷熱使池水乾枯。

28 overwhelming [ˌovɚˋhwɛlmɪŋ] *adj.* 壓倒一切的

Jason's proposal has been given overwhelming support.

傑森的提議獲得壓倒性的支持。

overwhelming majority 壓倒性多數

overwhelming odds 極大的優勢

an overwhelming sense of guilty 無比的罪惡感

29 deficiency [dɪˋfɪʃənsɪ] *n.* 缺乏；不足之數

Some children in Africa have a nutritional deficiency.

有些非洲小孩營養缺乏。

Some women suffer from iron deficiency in their diet.

有些女人飲食上缺乏鐵。

deficiency disease 營養缺乏症

主題 4

30 deny [dɪˋnaɪ] *vt.* 否定；拒絕相信

No one can deny the fact that smoking is harmful to health.

無人能否認抽菸傷身的事實。

The man denied murdering a woman at the party.

這人否認在派對上謀殺一名女人。

deny the existence of 否認……的存在

Unit 12

Space 太空

 Track 48

1 **universe** [ˋjunəˌvɝs] *n.* 宇宙，世界

The universe exists in space.

宇宙存在於太空。

be the center of one's universe 成為……最重要的人

a parallel universe 平行的宇宙

2 **formation** [fɔrˋmeʃən] *n.* 形成；構成；形成物

The soldiers marched in parade formation.

士兵以列隊的隊形行進。

3 **brood** [brud] *vi.* 憂悶地沉思；憂慮

Don't stay at home brooding the whole day long.

不要整天待在家裡鬱悶。

brood over the failure 擔憂失敗

4 **capacious** [kəˋpeʃəs] *adj.* 容量大的，寬敞的

The five-year-old child has a capacious memory.

五歲的小男孩有豐富的記憶力。

a capacious pocket 大口袋

5 **shapeless** [ˋʃeplɪs] *adj.* 無形的，無定形的

His ideas are creative but shapeless.
他的點子很有創意，但是不成形。

6 **stillness** [ˋstɪlnɪs] *n.* 寂靜，無聲 *adj.* 靜止的；寂靜的

The stillness of the night was rent by thunder.
雷鳴打破了夜晚的寂靜。

7 **estimate** [ˋɛstəˏmet] *vt.* 估計，評價 *n.* 估計

Richard is highly estimated among his friends.
理查在朋友中受到的評價很高。

The temple is estimated to be built at least 100 years ago.
這寺廟被估計至少是在一百年前所建。

8 **assume** [əˋsjum] *vt.* 假定；承擔；呈現

Steven did something wrong, and he will assume responsibility for it.
史帝芬做錯事，他願為此承擔責任。

I assumed that you'd gone to work because I didn't see your car.
因為我沒看到你的車，所以我想你應該去上班了。

it seems reasonable to assume that 假設……應是合理的……

主題 4

9 **zero** [ˋzɪro] *n.* 零；零點，零度

The probability of an industrial pollution control being reached is zero.
達成和工業污染控制的機率是零。

absolute zero 絕對零度

10 nowhere [`no,hwɛr] *adv.* 任何地方都不

The album was nowhere to be found.

這專輯無處可尋。

nowhere to go 無處可去

go nowhere 不成功；沒進步

11 comet [`kɑmɪt] *n.* 彗星

A comet is seen as a bright line in the sky.

彗星被看見向一條光亮的線劃過天空。

12 meteor [`mitɪɚ] *n.* 流星，大氣現象

A meteor shot across the starry sky.

流星劃過星空。

a meteor shower 流星雨

13 streak [strik] *n.* 條紋；光線；一陣子 *vi.* 形成線條；急駛

The cars streaked down the highway.

汽車在公路上疾駛而去。

streak of lightning 一束閃電

14 milky [`mɪlkɪ] *adj.* 牛奶的；乳白色的

I like my hot chocolate milky.

我愛喝加牛奶的熱可可。

milky complexion 牛奶膚色

Milky Way 銀河

15 firmament [`fɝməmənt] *n.* 蒼穹，天空

He rose his head and stared at the firmament.

他抬起頭，凝望著天空。

Kim is one of the rising stars in the economic firmament.

金是經濟界的未來之星。

16 **countless** [ˋkaʊntlɪs] *adj.* 數不盡的，無數的

There are countless stars in the sky.

天上有無數的星星。

17 **treacherous** [ˋtrɛtʃərəs] *adj.* 背判的；變化莫測的

He is treacherous to his friends.

他對他的朋友不忠。

The heavy snow has left the road treacherous.

大雪讓這路變得危險

18 **formidable** [ˋfɔrmɪdəb!] *adj.* 可怕的；難對付的

The house is grey, formidable and no one dares to go inside.

這房子陰灰又可怕，沒人敢進去。

主題 4

19 **expedition** [ˌɛkspɪˋdɪʃən] *n.* 探險；探險隊

The government sent an expedition to the North Pole.

政府派遣一支探險隊到北極。

on an expedition 去探險

20 **dangerous** [ˋdendʒərəs] *adj.* 危險的

The chemical is dangerous to humans.

這化學製品對人是有危害的。

21 **necessity** [nə`sɛsətɪ] *n.* 必要性；必然性

The manager emphasized the necessity for good ideas.

經理強調好點子的重要。

basic necessities 基本必需品

22 **search** [sɝtʃ] *vt.* *vi.* *n.* 在……中搜尋，搜查

The detective searched every room in the house for clues.

偵探為了找線索搜查了這房子的每一個房間。

fruitless search 徒勞無功的搜尋

23 **pioneer** [ˌpaɪə`nɪr] *n.* 先鋒 *vt.* 開闢

The designer is a pioneer of fashion.

這設計師是時尚的先驅。

a pioneer in the field of …領域的先驅

24 **spaceship** [`spes͵ʃɪp] *n.* 航太飛船

The spaceship is constructed by Russians.

這太空船是由俄羅斯人建造的。

spaceship Earth 太空船地球（地球就像太空船，依賴有限資源生存）

25 **alien** [`elɪən] *adj.* 外國的 *n.* 外國人

I ran into my classmate in the alien city.

我在他鄉的城市遇到同學。

The way of western life is totally alien to me.

西方生活對我來說是完全的性質不同的。

26 messenger ['mɛsndʒɚ] *n.* 送信者，信使

A messenger was attacked while taking the news to the soldiers at the front.

一名通訊員在去給前線士兵送消息時被攻擊了。

27 testimony ['tɛstə,monɪ] *n.* 證言，證明

Walt's testimony is important to the prosecution's case.

瓦特的證詞對這起訴案件很重要。

【同】evidence, declaration

28 unlock [ʌn'lɑk] *vt.* 開門，箱等；揭開

The curious boy unlocked the box to see what's inside.

好奇的小男孩打開箱子看看裡面是什麼。

unlock the secret of sth. 揭開…的秘密

29 disclose [dɪs'kloz] *vt.* 揭開；揭發；揭露

The jury has disclosed that two judges were under investigation.

陪審團透露有二名法官正受調查。

主題 4

30 alter ['ɔltɚ] *vt.* 改變，變更；改做

Have you altered your mind?

你改變主意了嗎？

His face hadn't altered much over the ten years.

他的臉在這十年並未改變很多。

alter ego 第二個我；心腹朋友

Leader 039

開啟職場主題字彙聯想力(MP3)

作　　者	力得編輯群
發 行 人	周瑞德
執行總監	齊心瑀
執行編輯	魏于婷
校　　對	編輯部
封面構成	高鍾琪

內頁構成	華漢電腦排版有限公司
印　　製	大亞彩色印刷製版股份有限公司
初　　版	2016 年 2 月
定　　價	新台幣 360 元
出　　版	力得文化
電　　話	(02) 2351-2007
傳　　真	(02) 2351-0887
地　　址	100　台北市中正區福州街 1 號 10 樓之 2
E - m a i l	best.books.service@gmail.com
網　　址	www.bestbookstw.com

港澳地區總經銷	泛華發行代理有限公司
地　　　　址	香港新界將軍澳工業邨駿昌街 7 號 2 樓
電　　　　話	(852) 2798-2323
傳　　　　真	(852) 2796-5471

國家圖書館出版品預行編目資料

開啟職場主題字彙聯想力 / 力得編輯群著. -- 初版. --
臺北市：力得文化, 2016.02
　面；　公分. -- (Leader；39)
ISBN 978-986-92398-7-5(平裝附光碟片)

1.英語 2.詞彙

　805.12　　　　　　104029310